CRAZY LOVE

HANNAH SMITH

First edition October 2023

ISBN: 978-0-6452802-3-4 (ebook)
ISBN: 978-0-6452802-2-7 (paperback)

Edited by Rachel Collins
Cover Design by ©Emily Wittig Designs

For my boys, Josh and Maxi.
Thank you for giving me my own kind of crazy love.

AUTHOR'S NOTE

This book contains sex scenes, profanity, themes of addiction, mild violence, sexual assault, death of parents (off-page), occasional on-page drug use, and is intended for audiences 18 years or older.

Crazy Love begins immediately after the epilogue in *Hazy Love* and contains many references and spoilers to the first book in the series.

I recommend reading the epilogue first as a refresher. If you haven't read *Hazy Love*, you can access the epilogue on my website: www.hannahsmithauthor.com

Happy reading!

1

KALI

NEVER HAVE I had to work this hard to get a man to make a move.

I've flirted all night, batted my eyelashes, puckered my lips and told all my best stories. My body is on a silver platter with neon signs pointing to 'go' and the god that is Anthony Bonetti still hasn't taken the bait.

The silence is palpable, broken only by the distant roar of the ocean beneath the nearby cliffs. That and my jittery foot tapping against the barstool. Across the moonlit kitchen island, Anthony leans back in his chair surveying me as I try my best to act as if my heart isn't banging in my ears. "Well?"

"I'm thinking."

The deep, gravelly inflection of his voice sends a shiver up my spine. His shiny gaze travels appreciatively across my exposed shoulders, dipping slightly to my collarbone. I'm not second-guessing his attraction to me, but I *am* questioning where his mind keeps wandering, where his thoughts go during his long pauses before asking or answering questions.

"There should be a time limit to the thinking, or you forfeit," I huff.

The left side of Anthony's mouth lifts into a lazy smile. "This game was your idea, Kali."

"And I should've set clearer rules." I lean forward onto the bench-top to get a better look at him, resting my chin in my hand. "It's been ten minutes—"

"It's been two."

I narrow my eyes. "Make a decision."

Anthony's eyes twinkle in the dim light. "Hair tie."

I can't pinpoint if it's relief or disappointment at allowing hair accessories to be included as clothing, as I breathe a quiet sigh and reach up to release my tangle of hair from its high bun, sweet relief rippling down my scalp as my hair springs free. "I'm surprised you didn't go with the shorts."

"I've got a thing for long hair. Good for grabbing onto." Anthony's eyes flash in the darkness and I fumble to collect the cards in front of us.

He's beating me at my own game, and he knows it. He's relishing the fact that I'm trying to get him to crack and he's purposely throwing out comments that trip me up.

I've done all the hard work tonight. After dinner with Anthony's brother Patrick, and my best friend Hazel, I insisted we go back to Patrick's new house overlooking the ocean at Burleigh Heads to check out the view. Anthony simply grinned at me. When Patrick and Hazel retired to bed, I suggested Anthony and I play UNO in lieu of a traditional deck of cards. I suggested we keep the lights off, letting the moonlight stream in from the windows to set the mood. I suggested we spice it up by adding the strip poker element. And I also suggested the *other* person got to choose which item of clothing to remove.

It was a fool-proof plan. I'd get to see Anthony with his shirt off, he'd see me half naked, and we'd ravage each other on the kitchen table, but it turns out, he's way better at UNO than I am and his refusal to request the removal of key items of clothing is his unique way of torturing me.

"Do you want to play another round?" I ask.

Anthony's gaze drifts to my breasts concealed behind a lace bra. We both know that if we go another round, and I lose, he's going to see me in a thong or get a full showing of my boobs.

He remains silent.

I smirk. "Scared, Bonetti?"

Anthony's mouth quirks as he reaches his hand out for the cards.

I hand them over and watch as he deftly shuffles with the skill and expertise of a dealer in a casino. "Where did you learn how to deal like that?"

"Prison."

I swallow, watching as Anthony keeps his focus on the cards, a pleasant ripple sounding as he feeds them into each other. "You've been to prison?"

He glances up at me. "Scared, Red?"

He's mimicking my earlier question, but I'm distracted by his choice of words to acknowledge it. "Red?"

"Yeah. I think it suits you."

I narrow my eyes at the insinuation in his tone, racking my brain for something I've said or done tonight that would make him call me Red, but I come up blank.

"You wouldn't be the first guy I've played strip poker with that's been to prison." I give him my sweetest smile.

My gaze drifts to Anthony's tattoos catching in the moonlight. There are so many pictures woven together, it's hard to make out what each of them is, especially in the darkness. A sailing ship, Latin words, a date in roman numerals on his inner wrist.

"Did you get your tattoos in prison too?"

Anthony nods, focusing on the cards. "Some of them. I got my first one at sixteen. They're addictive once you start."

"Any you regret? A koi carp? An ex's name?"

"Maybe if you started winning, you could find out."

"Ouch."

Anthony's Adam's apple rolls as he chuckles. "I've got a few names of people who mean something to me. No past lovers or koi carp though."

"Sensible choices."

"What about you, Red? You got any tattoos?"

"Just one." I smile sweetly. "You wanna see where?"

Anthony's gaze dips to my cleavage before darting away. "You're not going to have anywhere to hide when I kick your ass again. I'll find out soon enough."

"If I didn't know better, I'd say you were scared of me losing another round." I glance at him. "Where's the Anthony who was going to tie me up a few hours ago?"

Anthony leans forward. "I'm a man who likes to draw things out. Patience, remember?"

"I don't think I'll ever master the art of patience," I admit. "I get bored easily."

"That explains why you're single." Anthony winks, waiting for me to play my first card.

I roll my eyes, snapping my first card down. "I'm single because I want to be."

"When's the last time you had a boyfriend?"

I shrug. "I haven't had a serious boyfriend in years. I love love, and I appreciate beautiful relationships like Hazy and Patrizio's, but for me, the experience of dating lots of people and trying new things is much more exciting."

Anthony leans back, surveying me with intense focus. Fire rises from my chest onto my cheeks and unexpected heat courses through my limbs.

"I enjoy my freedom and the rush at the beginning of relationships more than being in one," I continue. "Most people do. They're just not honest with themselves about it. Love isn't high on my priority list."

Anthony snaps a card down. "I bet if you spent enough time with me, you'd fall in love."

I smile at him as I place another card down. "Unlikely."

Anthony places another card onto the pile, and I curse, reaching over to add a stack to my hand. "I'm incredibly patient," he reminds me.

"So, you've said."

We barely have enough time to continue with the conversation, because Anthony clears his hands of cards within seconds.

I lose, again.

Realising Anthony's probably going to delay suggesting I strip to my underwear; I plant my hands on the benchtop and push myself off my high-backed chair. I glance at Anthony, whose entire body has stilled.

Without hesitating, I unbutton my denim shorts, undo the zipper and slowly slide my shorts down my legs. Gently, I step out of them and remain standing before him in the semi-darkness. "Only bra and panties left."

Anthony stills as his molten gaze drags over my body. Adrenaline numbs my body as he rises from his chair, resembling a panther stalking its prey.

As he approaches, he becomes clearer. A tall, painted mass of lean muscle teases me from behind his sexy black clothing. His chiselled jaw tics, his blue eyes are swirling pools of heat. "I want to change the game we're playing. Something with higher stakes."

A chill ricochets through my body. "What are you thinking?"

Anthony's mouth lifts into a wicked smile. "I'm thinking you'll crack before I will."

Warmth creeps into my belly at the sight of his devilish expression.

"A bet," he says. "First one to cave to the other loses. Winner gets whatever they want. We state the stakes now. No questions asked."

The erratic rise and fall of my almost-bare chest should be embarrassing, but I'm too turned on to care. His body crowds my senses, and it takes every ounce of strength to keep my hands to myself. "What counts as caving?"

He grins. "I'm open to negotiating the terms, Red."

I stare at his full lips and blurt out the first thing that enters my brain. "A kiss. First person to kiss the other loses."

"What counts as a kiss?" Anthony lowers his head and presses his warm lips to my collarbone. My stomach bottoms out. "Does this count?"

His breath skates over my shoulder and it takes super-woman strength to not jump up and wrap my legs around his waist. "No. A kiss on the lips, with intent."

He leans back, a smugness to his expression. "First one to kiss the other on the lips, got it. What do you want if you win?"

My gaze hovers on the tattoos painted over his vascular neck. "If I win, you have to get a tattoo of my choosing."

Anthony's eyes flash with the promise of a challenge. "Deal. And if I win …" He pauses, stepping back and giving me some much-needed space to suck the oxygen out of the air. "If I win, I get to take you on a date."

I blink, my rush of sexual energy coming to a screaming halt. "What?"

"If I win, you go on a date with me."

I frown. "That's what you want? A date?"

Anthony watches me with narrowed eyes and nods.

"Why?" I ask, crossing my arms.

He shakes his head. "We said no questions asked. Your full participation on a real date."

I mull over his words. Our wants for winning this bet are vastly different. If his wanting to take me on a date has anything to do with my confessions about relationships and love, he'll be disappointed. He wouldn't be the first man to take on the challenge and fail miserably.

"If you're too chickenshit, Red, it's cool," he says, waving a hand dismissively.

I curve my lips into the sultriest smile I can muster before holding out my hand. "It's a deal, smartass."

As my hand slides into his, he yanks me forward, my hips colliding with his body. "Get dressed. I'm taking you home."

I don't hide my surprise. "What? Why?"

He turns away from me. "We're leaving in two minutes."

My skin tingles at the way he commands me. My inner feminist roars with rage. "Oh, I get it. Getting rid of temptation. Scared I'm going to win?"

Anthony whips around and pushes me back against the kitchen island. "I'm going to wipe the floor with you."

A gasp escapes my mouth as he runs his thumb down my hip, rubbing it across the spot where my tiny mandala tattoo sits. He latches onto my underwear, pulling it up with a snap on my hipbone and I squeak. "Even if you're making it incredibly difficult for me to keep it in my pants."

He spins and marches away, leaving me gasping for breath as if I've sprinted a race.

I look down and notice my G-string for the first time.

My bright, *red* G-string.

Well played, Bonetti.

2

ANTHONY

THE CAB of my truck isn't big enough to contain the thrumming electricity between the two of us. We've been locked inside for a couple of minutes and every bone in my body screams at the tension.

Kali must be feeling the same, because she keeps leaning across from the passenger seat, squeezing her tits together and doing her best to break me.

"It's not going to work, Red," I scoff.

It so will work. I'm about two seconds away from pulling this car to the roadside and bending her over the back seat.

"Party pooper." She sticks her tongue out before settling into her seat. I let out a quiet, deliberate breath to calm my racing heart as we continue the scenic drive to her house.

The ease at which we've settled into a rhythm mere hours after I showed up on her doorstep has me buzzing. As I suspected from the moment we met, she's self-assured and confident, and doesn't shy away from flirtation or conversation. She's funny. She gets my sense of humour. It's the first time I've felt this relaxed around a woman in years. She's also sexy as hell, like an Amazonian warrior with long dark-skinned legs and toned muscles rivalling a top-tier athlete.

"If you won't indulge me, tell me a story instead," she says, resting her elbow on the middle console. "We're trapped in a car for the next six minutes. Make it worth my while. Gimme something. How about a harsh truth? A dark secret? Those are always fun."

A flurry of thoughts race through my brain. The number of harsh truths and dark secrets pent up in my mind would be enough to bowl anyone over. The foster system, the number of brawls I've started and ended, my days as an addict, jail-time, Chloe …

I shake my head to clear it. Telling Hazel about my past had been easy. I've made solid progress at meetings and therapy. I own my mistakes and my past. The shame is part and parcel, but I've managed to spin a lot of it around thanks to the help of others.

But something stops me from spilling everything now.

"Right," she says after I remain silent for an embarrassingly long time. "How about I ask questions and you decide if you want to answer them or not?"

"Sure." I adjust my white-knuckled fists on the steering wheel. Kali notices but doesn't say anything.

"What's your favourite colour?"

I bark out a laugh of surprise and her face lights up. "Well, that was unexpected and obviously the answer is red." I wink at her, and she rolls her eyes.

"Favourite song?"

"*Break Stuff* by Limp Bizkit."

A snort escapes her nose. "Figures. Favourite subject at school?"

"Hmm. Does bashing people at lunch time count?"

"Were you that bad?" she asks.

"I was a dick," I admit, slowing to a stop at a set of lights. "I couldn't concentrate at school. Used to have a crazy temper."

"You don't strike me as the type to have a temper."

"I've mellowed in my adult years," I reply. Prison time, trauma, therapy and Narcotics Anonymous could either send one over the edge or calm a man to the point of being *too* Zen. I'll take the latter any day of the week.

"Are you excited about your apprenticeship?" she asks.

I glance at her before responding. She's turned in the passenger seat to face me, one of her legs curled underneath her as she waits for my answer. Streetlights flicker over her body as we make our way towards her house, and when I catch her gaze, she gives me a bright smile.

"Yeah, I am." It's a battle to focus on the road ahead instead of her. "I may be one of the oldest apprentices known to man, but it'll be nice to work with my hands. As much as I enjoyed playing Patty's bodyguard and getting involved in undercover police work, carpentry is more my scene."

"As a true crime fan, I'm jealous you got to be involved in a real investigation," Kali says. "But how on Earth were you even *allowed* in a real investigation?"

I chuckle. "Civilians are involved more than you think. Plus, they wanted Patty and Patty would only work with me. Well, he wanted to keep babysitting me, I guess."

Kali's gaze burns into the side of my head and my thoughts drift back to all the truths I want to spill but am too cowardly to admit. I wonder how much she knows about my past. I wonder what Hazel spilt to her best friend.

My brother's been watching me like a hawk for the past few years, but I don't blame him for it. If anything, I'm used to it. He's slowly giving me more and more space, and our check-ins are becoming less frequent, but I know I'm on his mind more than he lets on.

I tense my knuckles around the steering wheel again as we

enter Kali's neighbourhood. No matter how much work I think I've done on dealing with my demons, something dark always sits under the surface, waiting to explode.

Change the subject.

"What about you?" I ask. "Have you always been into fitness?"

Kali smiles. "Dancing and gymnastics, yeah. My grandmother made sure I attended every class and every competition. I found Pilates once I left school and haven't looked back."

"It shows." I throw her an exaggerated appreciative glance and she grins wider. "Did you win at these dancing comps of yours?"

"Of course," Kali says, without irony. "I destroyed the competition. I'm great at winning."

I slow the car to a stop outside Kali's house and pull the handbrake on. Unnerved by the effect her stare has on me, I shift my entire body in the driver's seat. "And I bet you suck at losing."

"Gracious losers are never fully in it," she says. "If you're all-in, armed to the teeth competing, the loss should hurt like hell. It should be all over your face and bleeding out of you."

"And you're an all-in type of woman."

Kali lifts her head and grins. "Absolutely."

"Except for relationships, right?" I ask. "What was it you said? You enjoy the freedom and rush at the beginning of relationships more than being in one?"

Kali's smile falters. "Yeah, so what? I'm *all-in* on not being monogamous. I prefer that above a committed relationship."

A snicker slips from my mouth. "Whatever you need to tell yourself."

As a woman who appears able to take any sort of ribbing, the mere mention of her feelings on love and relationships elicits something unexpected.

A shadow glimmers across her face.

Her eyes harden.

Oh. I've hit a nerve.

"Excuse me?" she seethes.

Unlucky for her, I stopped sugar-coating my words a long time ago. "I'm saying that maybe you're not *all-in* on monogamy because you're afraid of commitment, because you fear love."

Kali scoffs. "Did you say you were *in* therapy or a therapist?"

"I've had enough therapy for the both of us, Red," I murmur. "And I can tell you right now, you ain't fooling me."

"Thanks for your concern, *doctor*," she snaps. "But I'm not trying to fool anyone. Love is great. I just happen to enjoy my life as it is. Carefree and uncomplicated."

I take note of how she holds herself. Tense, defensive, ready to claw at my throat. Instead of backing down, my mouth opens before my brain catches up. "My therapist would have a field day with you." It was a dick thing to say, but my skin pulses with excitement all the same.

Kali blinks several times before setting her jaw steady. She scoops up her bag and furiously snaps the door handle, stepping outside the car.

"It's fun getting under your skin," I call after her.

She ducks down to look at me, her brown eyes alight with fury. "You're not getting under *anything.*"

"We'll see. The bet is still on and I'm no quitter."

Kali slams the door in my face, and I chuckle.

Damn. I like that woman.

I like her a lot.

3

KALI

I DIDN'T CRY when my dad died.

Not when I found out, nor when I realised, he was never coming home. I didn't cry when I thought about how one minute he was here, and the next, he was gasping for his final breaths as his young heart betrayed him, leaving me and my mother alone to fend for ourselves. Not one single tear.

My therapist at the time said there could be a variety of reasons for that. She gave me three of her best educated guesses:

One, I was experiencing trauma, and my brain was protecting me by suppressing extreme emotions, choosing to numb the pain to help me survive.

Two, I was trying to be strong for my mother, who instantaneously changed the minute she heard the news, barely able to hold it together long enough to take her anti-depressants and finish a bottle of wine before noon.

Or three, her favourite of the options. The one where she'd tilt her head and give me a sympathetic smile, her eyes warm and understanding, and full of *pity*. Number three, the gold standard option, was that I, seven-year-old Kalina Cooper, was angry.

I was angry at dad for leaving; angry at the world for taking him. I was angry at everyone who got to keep their fathers. Who got to share memories and achievements, Christmases and birthdays. But mostly, I was angry at my mother, who failed to act like one the minute she got the life-changing phone call.

I wouldn't say I'm an angry person *now*. I've done a lot of work to get to a good place. My Mimi has her doubts about that. She thinks I'm still suppressing anger, although she prefers to say I'm 'passionate' instead of angry.

"Are you still seeing that boy?" she asks through my earphones. "What's his name ..."

I scoop up my bag of belongings, shivering as I drape a small towel around my shoulders. The water's still warm in April but getting out of the ocean when there's a chill in the air sucks ass. "Which boy?"

"You know, lovely Meg's cousin."

"You mean, Alex?"

Alex and I had a few months of cute dates and great sex last year. I surprised myself with how much I let go of my carefree stance on relationships, to a degree. We were never official, but I loved spending time with him. You know that honeymoon, mad rush, endorphin-driven period? No wonder I'm not into monogamy. That initial rush is addictive as all hell. In the end, we fizzled to nothing. I'm not sure why.

That's a lie.

After I started receiving gifts from Anthony, I got distracted. I thought about him too much. I imagined what he'd taste like and freaked myself out, because what you imagine in your brain is never as good as the real thing.

Ever since Friday night, I've thought about him even more. Almost obsessively. Thinking about the way he carries himself, re-living the jokes he told. His *cheekiness*. He doesn't mince his words, much like me.

I drag my thoughts back to the present. "Alex and I stopped seeing each other a while ago, Mimi."

My grandmother hums to herself and I imagine her eyes narrowing. Mimi is no stranger to my dating of multiple men. She's never been bothered by my dating habits, often putting it down to 'a generation she doesn't understand'.

"How is the other young man doing? The man who sends you gifts. Antony."

My stomach does an involuntary lurch as I make my way up the sand dunes. "It's *Anthony*."

"I prefer Antony."

I laugh. "I'll let him know."

"How is he doing?"

I smile on instinct before biting it back in annoyance. "Good. He's moved here from Sydney, and I went out with him on Friday night. He's funny, but obnoxious and doesn't know where to draw the line."

"Doesn't sound familiar at all," Mimi says.

"I know I can be overbearing, but this guy made judgement calls on my life. He's a bit of a wanker." I kick the sand beneath my feet, remembering his comments about my fear of commitment.

"Hush Kalina, your language. What would Baba say if he could hear you?"

I chuckle. "Baba used to smoke weed with me and let me say the 'f' word. He wouldn't be mad at me."

My grandmother tuts under her breath again. "How is Hazel?"

"Madly in love. A heartbeat away from having your grandbabies."

I hear Mimi gasp with excitement. "That makes me happy."

"Hazel's offspring is the closest you're getting to grandchildren any time soon. I'm too busy enjoying my life to get caught up in that life."

My grandmother's voice softens. "Kalina. I don't care about grandbabies. I care about you and your happiness. You should use the money you have to do something for yourself. Spend it on something for you. Invest in your future."

She always brings up the goddamn money. "I know, Mimi."

"Think about it, Kalina. You're nearly thirty. Now's the time to make a plan. Promise me you'll think about it."

We both know I'm not touching the goddamn money. "Sure."

I hear my grandmother sigh as I reach the footpath that will lead me home. "Kali, don't spend your life floating through it."

"I'm not," I groan. "I've travelled. I've been to university, albeit briefly, but I gave it a crack. I try everything once. I'm not floating through life. I'm *experiencing* it."

"You've experienced so much. You *feel* so much," she replies. "But sometimes your passion gets in the way of you experiencing other emotions. I worry your passion will be your downfall."

It's my turn to sigh. I know what Mimi's about to say before the words leave her lips. "Don't ever stop being passionate, but don't let it get in the way of experiencing real joy."

I end the conversation quickly after that and hang up with a sigh, continuing towards home in a much darker mood than when I left.

Why? Why does she have to always mention the money?

It's as if Mimi has a quota to hit or something. Every second conversation lately has been about me making plans with the money, investing the money, *doing something with THE MONEY.*

My phone buzzes with my friend Rocco's face appearing on the screen. A call from him is almost certain to cheer me up, even if it's unexpected. The fact Rocco is calling me before nine o'clock on a Sunday morning is nothing short of surprising.

He's usually hungover and in bed with his latest conquest after a Saturday night.

"Hey."

"Thank God you answered. I am freaking out!"

I roll my eyes. "What's happened this time? Your boyfriends caught onto each other, didn't they? I told you; you need to be smarter about how you date."

"I ran into Weird Michelle last night!" Rocco cries. "Ow! My head. Ugh, anyway I totally forgot until now. She told me the gym's been bought out by new owners. They signed a deal at the close of business on Friday."

A sinking sensation settles in my stomach, my pace slowing on the footpath. "Are you sure? Are you sure she wasn't just being Weird Michelle?"

Rocco lets out an exasperated sigh. "She was wasted, but there's *no way* she was lying. She said she was out drinking her sorrows away and said everyone's getting let go *tomorrow*. They're bringing in new staff and rebranding everything! Kali, can they do that?"

I struggle to find the words to respond as I register what Rocco's saying. The gym that's been my home for three years, the place where I've come into my own as a Pilates instructor, is about to kick me out with less than a day's notice.

"I don't know, Rocco," I finally say. "Did you call Andrew?"

"As if that coward's going to answer my calls," Rocco spits. "If he wasn't going to give us a bit of goddamn notice, he sure as shit ain't going to answer the day before this big announcement. He's probably halfway to Mexico by now."

If what Rocco is saying is true, I'm going to be an unemployed, commitment-phobe in twenty-four hours' time. Not that the commitment-phobe part bothers me, but it's another label I don't need that keeps popping into my head.

"I'm going to make some more calls," Rocco says. "Keep your phone on you. I'll let you know what I find out."

"Thanks." I hang up before slowing to a complete stop in the middle of the street.

No matter what beacon of hope tries to shine right now, I can already feel it in my bones that Weird Michelle was telling the truth.

Eventually, I make it to the pathway leading to my front porch, trying not to let a million emotions spill over into too much *passion*.

Stomp, stomp, stomp.

Both phone calls upset my Sunday morning plans, but there's no point in getting worked up, yet. Mimi means well and Rocco might be wrong, or at the very least, exaggerating.

Stomp, stomp, stomp.

"Having a bad day?"

I whip my head up with a start and my vision fills with sweat-soaked, tattooed muscles. Anthony's broad, lean body fills the doorway, his arm leaning against the frame as he wipes his hands on a cloth. A small, unsure smile plagues the corners of his mouth.

The dark cloud hanging over my head dissipates. "What?"

Anthony juts his chin towards me. "You stomped up that pathway like it screwed you over."

"If this pathway had screwed me over, it'd be getting a lot worse than a few angry steps."

His lips curve upwards. "Nice to see you again, Red."

I cock my head, an inexplicable energy simmering in my chest. "And you, Dr Bonetti. At my home, no less."

Anthony chuckles. "Man, I really did a number on you, didn't I?"

"Oh, yes. You've cured me of all my trauma with your

ground-breaking insights. What do I owe you for your invaluable time?"

"That's why I'm here. To collect payment for my services."

My cheeks flush at the insinuation in his tone. "Payment?"

Anthony's fleeting gaze dips to the rest of my body. "Feel like caving, Red?"

Yes. "Never. What are you doing in my house?"

Right on cue, Hazel pops her head around Anthony's shoulder. "Hey Kali, did Anthony tell you he's making me a new desk?" She gives me a big smile. "How good is it knowing carpenters? I've set him up in the garage. Once he's done, I thought we could clear it out and use it for its main purpose. You know, parking our cars in there instead of storing our junk." Hazel's phone buzzes in her hand and she steps away as quickly as she arrived.

I turn back to Anthony. "How long is this desk going to take?"

He screws his face up in thought. "You mean, how long am I going to hang around your house, shirtless and irresistible? Not sure. Could be weeks. Could be tough on you."

I step up onto the porch and lean into Anthony, who holds his ground in the doorway. "Two can play at that game. Don't get ahead of yourself."

We hold each other's gaze, daring the other to move first. Before I can overthink it, I run a finger down the sweat glistening on the right side of his chest. I glance at him through my eyelashes as my finger gently trails all the way down to his waistline. Without breaking my gaze, I slowly lift my whole finger into my mouth and suck back to the tip.

Pure victory sings in my chest as Anthony swallows, his gaze darkening as he watches me lick my lips, relishing the taste of salt and sawdust and *him* on my tongue.

I make to move past him, but he drops an arm across the frame. Our faces are inches apart and his warm, minty breath trails into my nostrils. My stomach tightens as my eyes are drawn to his, his blue iris's hypnotising as he stares down at me.

"It's good to see you again, *Kali*." The way he utters my name sends a volt of electricity through my body.

"I wish I could say the same," I lie. My eyes flicker to Anthony's full lips, his white teeth peeking out from behind a small, sexy smile.

I push past him, so I don't cave.

So, I don't buckle under his gaze and grab his face.

So, I don't kiss him when every fibre of my being wants to.

4

ANTHONY

I GRIN as I watch Kali saunter away, her hips swaying from side to side. She *knows* I'm watching her. Her confidence is one of the sexiest things about her. Her resolve for her own beliefs and morals. She's so self-assured about so much stuff. Some guys find that intimidating, but I think it's a massive turn-on.

"What are you smiling about?" Hazel rounds the corner with an iced glass of water held out to me.

"Admiring your best friend from a distance," I admit, taking it from her with a wink.

Hazel rolls her eyes. "She's going to make you work for it, you know."

"No complaints here. I relish a good challenge."

Kali disappears into her bedroom, and I sigh with appreciation, which earns me a knock at the back of my head. "Ow!"

"None of that when I'm here."

I cast her a mocking glare. "You're as bad as Patty."

I don't know why I suggested the bet in the first place or why I think I can last much longer than I already have. It took a hell of a lot of willpower not to throw her against the wall of the porch as she pouted up at me. It took a hell of a lot of willpower to not grab her face and kiss her, to claim her mouth like it belonged to me.

I've been with my fair share of women in my time. Some fleeting and forgettable, some who I loved and will never forget, some who broke me in more ways than I knew were possible. But something about Kali lights a flame within me that's been out for a long time.

"The house is off-limits to your shenanigans," Hazel says, heading into the garage.

I follow her as I sip my water. "Why?"

"Because I don't want to walk out and see you and Kali having sex on the kitchen counter."

"Now *that* is an image I'm going to replay over and over tonight."

Hazel gags and slaps my arm. "Don't be that guy."

"Hate to break it to you, Jonesy, but I *am* that guy."

Hazel shakes her head before taking in the workshop explosion in her garage. My power tools are lined up against the wall and planks of wood scatter the sheeted floor. It took a good half hour to push Hazel and Kali's boxes of crap to the side before I could even set up. "Thank you for doing this."

"It's nothing." I tip the rest of the water down my throat and wipe my mouth. "But you can repay me by getting your girl to crack first."

Hazel narrows her eyes at me. "You're both crazy."

"Thank you. She's a wildcat, as I suspected." I hesitate before lowering my voice. "You didn't tell her about ... you know ..."

Hazel offers me a kind smile. "What's happened in your past are not my stories to tell, Anthony."

"Right."

"You wish I had told her, don't you? So, you didn't have to?"

I nod, unabashed. "It's not a conversation that comes up over coffee."

"I know, but it's not my place to tell her," Hazel continues. "And I know it must be hard to be vulnerable with someone again, but Kali is the most accepting, fiercely loving person in the world. You should give her the chance to hear all of it. From *you*."

I'm not sure that's true. What Kali and I are doing feels a lot like fooling around with off-the-Richter sexual chemistry. Maybe she doesn't need to know. Maybe it'll fizzle out before we get to all the heavy stuff.

"My story is a downer," I say.

Hazel fishes the glass out of my hand. "Or is it uplifting because you came out of it?"

A comfortable silence settles between us as I mull over her words. Is she right? I've spent the last few years learning to own my mistakes, but it doesn't mean there aren't times when thinking about them makes me want to vomit. Especially when there's a beautiful, intimidating woman involved.

"Stop overthinking. It'll give you wrinkles." Hazel raises her hand and rubs against the frown lines between my eyes. "Trust me. I've got hundreds of them."

As she heads back out of the room and leaves me alone with my thoughts, I play out different scenarios in my mind. Different scenarios on how to talk to Kali about something serious. How to explain to Kali the darkest and most shameful parts of my past.

And wondering why the hell I want to spill my secrets to a woman I barely know.

5

KALI

"I AM SCREWED."

Weird Michelle had told the truth. When I walked into the gym on Monday morning, there were strangers standing in the foyer, as well as security, advising all contractors they had ten minutes to collect their belongings and vacate the gym. We weren't even allowed to talk to any members.

"No, you're not," Hazel scolds me.

"I'm a twenty-eight-year-old woman with no job, which means no income to pay rent, buy food or get coffee."

Hazel soothes my arm. "You've got this, Kali. You've got qualifications and we live in the fitness hub of the entire state. Everybody here is constantly looking for instructors."

"You *do* remember how long it took me to find a studio that didn't suck, right?"

Hazel winces. Oh, she remembers. It took years of hopping around different gyms, studios and bootcamps, trying to find one that had consistent clientele, flexible hours and a manager who wasn't an arrogant prick. Andrew's a money-grabbing weasel, but at least he's fair. I wouldn't know where to even start a new search.

"Let's look at this logically and in a non-dramatic way," Hazel says, shifting to sit on the coffee table in front of me.

"How dare you insinuate I'm dramatic."

Hazel ignores me. "First, you've got me. I'm not going to let anything bad happen to you. Even if we have to split my income and survive off instant noodles. We've done it before; we can do it again."

I laugh at the fond memory of us living in a tiny studio apartment ten years ago, cracking open money tins and desperately scraping together any amount of coin to get us through another week.

"Number two," Hazel continues. "You've got your shit together. You have savings which will tide you over and ... you know."

My eyes shift to look at her serious expression and I frown. "What?"

"You have a buttload of cash sitting there, Kali."

I groan. "You sound like Mimi."

"That is one of the highest compliments you could pay me," Hazel replies. "If you got over yourself, you could take some time off and not work for a while."

"Get over myself?" I gasp. "That hurts."

"I'm serious, Kali."

"Maybe I could beg for my job back," I mutter. "Convince the new owners I'd be an asset."

"We both know that's not an option. You're too good to grovel."

"Excellent point," I agreed. "What I should do is open my own studio and run those peanuts out of business."

Hazel perks up. "You could do that."

I smile. "Buy a place and fit it out all fancy with the changes I want and make their members come to me with some very unsubtle advertising."

Hazel smiles, her eyes flickering with excitement. "Kali. You should do that."

I snort. "I'm joking."

Hazel jumps back onto the couch beside me. "I'm not! Kali, why don't you open your own studio?"

"Where would you like me to start, Hazy?"

"Why not? Kali, you have money sitting there."

I scowl at her. I'm not touching the money and she knows it.

"Would you get over your pride and think about this for a second?" she snaps.

"I liked you better when you were heartbroken. You were nicer to me then."

"You've got money sitting there you can use. Your clients would find you because they love you, and word travels fast. Ooh, ooh! Patrick could help you find a space!"

I see the cogs turning in my best friend's brain, her eyes sparkling. "Hazy—"

"Kali, this is perfect. You've got nothing to lose."

"Except money and pride."

"You're not touching the money anyway! Who cares if it doesn't work out?"

"Did you not hear the part about my pride?"

But Hazel's not listening to me. She taps away at her phone, bouncing in her seat. "I could design your logo and signage. We'd have to brainstorm some names. K.C. Fitness? No, that reminds me of KFC. How about something like the Pilates Pod, or Plank Palace? No, that's like a Chinese restaurant's name. I think I'm hungry again."

I sink into the couch, watching her face light up. Could I do this? Is that even an option? I wouldn't have the first clue about how to run a business, let alone start my own from scratch. And what if I did manage to do it? The fitness industry is fickle and once word starts to spread that I've started my own business, it would only be a matter of time before the bigger organisations tried to take me down. I've seen that happen first-hand. Not only that, I've also seen countless businesses close in quick succession. All these people have dreams and convince themselves they'll be different. That their idea will work. Six months later, their shit's cleared out and there's a 'for lease' sign on the door.

I open my mouth to complain about this to my best friend, but her eyes are wide with excitement, and I don't have the heart to break her spirit.

6

ANTHONY

Do you know how hard it is to avoid wandering to the kitchen for glasses of water in the hopes I'll walk past a particular woman? I have a two-litre canteen to drink out of in my truck and I left it there on purpose when I arrived. I wanted to traipse to and from Hazel and Kali's kitchen on the off-chance I'd bump into the fiery temptress. Other than greeting her when she arrived home and a brief exchange of smirks and scowls while the girls ate dinner, I haven't seen her.

When my watch clicks over to nine o'clock, I know it's time to wrap it up. I might have spent a lot of the evening looking out for Kali, but most of it I spent lifting, measuring, sawing and drilling as I started the desk for Jonesy. My muscles ache and I know I need to get home before sleep hits me like a freight train.

"Calling it a night?"

Her voice is warm honey to my ears. Kali's leaning against the door frame, her gaze wandering over my makeshift workstation. My tools sit neatly on the workbench I brought with me, scraps of debris littering the space underneath. Wood panels lay on the floor and prop up against the wall.

"It's way past my bedtime." I sweep the remnants of today's mess into a pile at my feet.

Kali glances at her watch. "It's nine o'clock."

"I don't have this beautiful complexion by staying up late and smoking doobies," I reply, nodding at the poorly concealed joint in her hand.

Kali's tanned complexion flushes. "Half the personal trainers on the Gold Coast do ketamine on weekends. I'm allowed a bit of marijuana now and then. Besides, *technically* I'm unemployed now, so I don't answer to anybody."

I chuckle. "I'm not judging, Red."

Kali seems pleased with that response and heads across the room to the open garage door, leaning against the outside wall and retrieving a lighter from her pocket.

Memories of skipping school to buy weed off the local dealer flash before my eyes. It was harmless fun back then. Little did I know how complicated and dark my using journey was going to become.

"Jonesy said you're thinking of opening your own Pilates studio?" I prompt to change topics. Talking about vices is not a path I want to go down right now.

A sigh escapes Kali's mouth before she takes a drag of her joint. She holds her breath for a few seconds before exhaling, a thick plume of smoke disappearing into the night sky. "Did she?"

"It's a good idea."

Kali's eyes dart to me. "Why do you say that?"

"Because you don't strike me as the type of woman who should work for anyone other than themselves." I continue to pack away my things, wiping down the surfaces covered in dirt and particles. "You get to be your own boss, make your own rules, make your own schedule. It takes courage. I may not know a lot about you, Red, but I can tell you're brave."

Kali dips her head in apparent shyness, and something

swells in my chest. "Thanks, but I wouldn't say I'm brave." Kali looks back up at the star-studded sky, blurred thanks to the light pollution of the city. "I wouldn't even know where to start."

There's a vulnerability about her I hadn't noticed until now. In our brief interactions, she's been the go-getter, takes-what-she-wants, Kali, but now, I see a woman on the precipice of big life changes and unsure how to take it.

"If it was easy, everybody would do it," I say.

Kali looks back at me and smiles. "Did your therapist tell you that one?"

"You don't need a therapist to know that one. It's the oldest in the book."

Kali peers at me with squinted eyes. "Can I ask you something?"

"Sure."

"Why do you see a therapist?" she asks. "I mean, I think it's great, but you're the first man I've met who's so open about going to therapy."

My mouth twists as I try to find the words to explain in the simplest terms. The other night in the car, my brain couldn't settle on how to even start telling Kali the truth about my past. The familiar sensation of panic rises in my throat, but I stamp it down with a clearing of my throat.

"I wasn't always keen on it," I admit. "Thought it was for people to cry about their feelings and get pat on the back for it. Turns out, it was a huge part of me turning my life around. I've got no shame in telling anybody that."

Kali tilts her head. "What made you want to turn your life around?"

I do my best to offer her a smile, but it falls flat. "When I win the bet and you go on a date with me, I promise I'll tell you."

Kali quirks an eyebrow. "Your straight, white-male confidence is almost comical."

I chuckle, dusting off my hands. "That's me for the night." I collect my phone and keys off the bench and walk over to where Kali still leans against the outside wall. Her eyes are on me, but I don't know what she's thinking. When I reach her, her breathing changes and her chest rises and falls, her dark hair flies off from its high bun, and I can see her high cheekbones covered in a moonlit sheen. She is fiercely beautiful. It's terrifying how much power she holds with one stare.

This bet becoming confusing was not part of my plan. One minute we're bickering, the next we're practically tearing each other's clothes off with our eyes.

"For what it's worth, I think you'd be great at it."

Kali frowns. "At therapy?"

I smile. "At running your own studio. You can do anything you set your mind to. I know a lot of people say that, but I reckon it applies to you. And if you need any other reasons to go for it, I could help you with the carpentry side of things. I'm good with my hands, remember?"

My gaze dips to the toned strip of her midriff poking out from her tank top. I reach down and let my finger trail across it, internally cheering as Kali gasps. The joint clasped in her fingers falls to the ground, forgotten. Leaning in, I inhale her coconut scent, my nose skimming across her jaw as my breath puffs onto her neck. I hear her swallow. "Good night, Red."

I step back and hop into my truck before I pitch a tent in my pants. As I turn out of the driveway, I can't help but look in the rear-view mirror to see Kali grinning to herself.

7

KALI

"WHAT DO you think I should do?"

I place the cup and saucer on the dining room table in front of Mimi, before spinning the teapot handle in my direction. She taps my hand. "I can pour my own tea, Kalina. I'm not useless."

I tap her withered hand back. "Stop being so stubborn. Let me pour the tea when I visit."

She huffs under her breath but concedes. I pour us both a cup, before sitting across from her at the table. "Well? Any words of wisdom for me?"

I've rattled off my potential business idea to my grandmother and she's given me zero indication of what she's thinking. She's given me the same face she always does when listening to stories. Eyes narrowed in suspicion, like everyone's up to something. She barely moved a muscle as I told her.

"I can't tell you what to do Kalina," she says, finally.

"I'm asking for advice Mimi," I reply. "You're almost ninety. Surely, you've got some magic pearls of wisdom hidden in those wrinkles."

"I might be old Kalina, but don't think I won't make you pay for that." A smile threatens at her mouth before she takes a sip of her drink. I wait for her to say more.

I know my Mimi. Never one to rush to solve anyone's problems. Never one to shy away from tough love. Mimi's a firm believer that people already have the answers, they just need help pulling them out.

"You've got a great opportunity in front of you," she muses. "If you don't take this opportunity, what's the alternative?"

"Moving back in with you," I reply dryly.

Mimi smiles. "I would take you back in a heartbeat, but not because you fear a new adventure. You've never feared anything. Always so passionate. Too passionate." Mimi mutters the last few words to herself. She's been saying that my entire life. "What does Anthony think of all this?"

I choke on my tea and spend the next few seconds coughing and banging my fist against my chest. Mimi raises an eyebrow as she waits for me to compose myself.

"He thinks I should do it," I say, clearing my throat again. Mimi's eyes narrow and my cheeks heat.

"Hmm."

"Hmm? That's all you have to say? *Hmm?*"

Mimi picks up a teaspoon and stirs her tea. "If you open this studio, how much will it cost?"

"A lot. Starting a business is expensive. There's location, permits, equipment, renovation costs, staff ... it's a lot."

Mimi looks at me deadpan. "You have the money, Kalina." I suck the air between my teeth at her triumphant expression. "The Kali I know wouldn't be thinking twice about this. I'm surprised you're not knocking down doors and drafting plans already. Something's holding you back. If this is about the money, Kalina, you need to put your pride aside."

Despite the way her words bristle, I know she's right. As usual. Something *is* holding me back. I never think on things for this long. I make decisions with ease, because I usually know what I want. The reality is I've spent the past couple of days searching for someone to tell me this whole thing is a bad idea, so it'll be easier to not take a chance and I won't have to touch my inheritance.

And why don't I want to touch my inheritance? Because, as Mimi beautifully pointed out, I'm too proud.

Later that night, I'm tossing and turning, playing my conversation with Mimi on repeat.

My pride has got in the way of a lot of things in my life. It's as if I have this innate need to prove that I don't need anyone else's help. My career, purchasing my first car, travelling the world, were all achieved without a cent from anyone else. I wanted to prove to myself and everyone else that I didn't need a handout from anyone. That having two absent parents would never stop me from achieving what I wanted. That I didn't *need* my parents or their money.

I flex my fingers, cracking the knuckles as I stare at my darkened ceiling. I miss my parents. My faded memories of us as a happy family are ones I cling to dearly. I'm not exactly sure when I hardened at the mere mention of them or when I decided I'd never touch the inheritance. Lying here in the darkness, it doesn't make sense.

I have a heap of money from my parents that could help me in so many ways, and I'm not touching it out of stubbornness. I roll my eyes at the ceiling. Even admitting that to myself gives me the ick, but it's true, not spending it isn't going to prove anything.

My stomach churns with anticipation. It reminds me of the night before something big, like Christmas or a big dance concert. I've lost my job, plain and simple, and now have the opportunity to make some real decisions on what to do next.

Do I want to work for another gym and spend the next few years building new connections, new friends and complaining about their set-up and rules I have no control over? Where would that lead me? In a couple of years, I'll be thirty, with no direction or purpose and nothing that's mine.

Until I lost my job, I didn't realise how badly I wanted something to call mine. I don't own a house or have any assets apart from my RAV4, and she's bound to break down any day now. Permanently.

If this is about the money, Kalina, you need to put your pride aside.

Bloody, Mimi. She's always right.

I whip my phone out and unlock it. I've made the decision about what to do next before I even pull up his number.

8

KALI

"WHAT DO YOU THINK?"

I stare at Patrick, and he grins, pushing the roller door the entire way up to let more light in. Dust clouds swirl in the sunlight. "It's got potential, trust me."

The smell of musty dampness hits me in the face, and I screw my nose up on instinct. The space in front of me looks as if a hurricane tore through it ten years ago and it hasn't been touched since.

I follow him inside. The makeshift walls covered in graffiti are collapsing. It used to be an office space a lifetime ago, with a dilapidated counter to the right and a hallway of darkness taking you to the back of the room.

"Is this place even safe to use?" I ask, peering around to the left where a kicked in door leads to a broken toilet.

Patrick chuckles. "My guy came and did a check and said you couldn't have anyone in here in its current condition."

I eye the filth and grime lining the walls. "Because it's a death trap?"

Patrick smiles. "He's already lodged a building approval. He says despite the work it needs, it's structurally sound and has fire safety." Patrick nods to the fire alarms in the high ceiling. "Whilst there are bugs around, it won't be hard to get a pest control guy, and there are no termites. Plumbing is good and it meets the minimum energy and water efficiency standards."

With my arms crossed across my chest, I take a further step inside and peep along the makeshift hallway, which is filled with debris.

"This lot is in an approved council zone for a gym, so you don't need planning permission. It's an industrial area, which means you're unlikely to piss anyone off with loud music, and you've got ample parking."

Check. Check. Check again. All things I'd need for this to have a chance of being successful. I shuffle along the hallway, pulling my t-shirt over my nose to block the stench and kicking litter out of my way. Mold lines the skirting boards, splintered in some parts, completely dislodged in others. Every piece of furniture in here is broken, all the light fixtures are destroyed and not one wall has been spared vandalism. Patrick mentioned squatters used it before the real estate company came and put a deadlock on it. I do my best to imagine what it would look like once the walls are knocked down, a slick coat of cream paint on the walls, hanging lights and potted plants.

I'm having trouble visualising.

"I got you a good deal, if you want to take it." Patrick hands me a business card as I make my way back to him. The scribble on the back stares back at me and I realise it's half of what others have offered.

I gape at him. "How did you ...?"

Patrick winks and gives me a kind smile. "I pulled some strings. Listen, Kali. I know I've only known you a short while, but I think what you're doing is smart and courageous. I really think you can do something great here."

My heart swells. A year ago, this man was a stranger to me

and now, he's giving me the gentle encouragement I need to take a leap and do something big.

"You're kind of like a dad, sometimes." Patrick's smile falters and I smile back, throwing my arms around his waist, squeezing his body to mine. "Thank you."

He's clearly surprised because he freezes, but I don't care. He's gone out of his way to do something nice for me.

When he finally returns the embrace, I give him a squeeze and free him from his awkwardness.

"Where do I sign?"

UNKNOWN

Please stop sending unsolicited nudes

ME

I'm blocking whoever this is

UNKNOWN

This is the sexiest man you've ever met

ME

Impossible. I've never met Timothee Chalamet

BONETTI

That boy is 12

ME

How dare you. But also, I'm impressed you know who Timothee Chalamet is

BONETTI

I hear you signed some serious paperwork today

ME

Patrizio could've kept that to himself

BONETTI

Jonesy told me

ME

Is nothing sacred? How did you get my
number?

BONETTI

See previous reply

ME

Well yes, I've signed on the dotted line of
death. Here goes nothing

BONETTI

Congrats Red. Never doubted you for a second

I grin to myself.

9

KALI

"YOU HAVE GOT to be kidding me."

Meg turns to me with her face screwed up in disgust as I flick the light to the warehouse on. Rachel lets out a chortle of laughter and steps inside, followed closely by Hazel. Now that the power's hooked up, renovations can start. My friends offered to come down to see my space and help me get started on clearing the mess out. Meg, somewhat begrudgingly.

She's donned her very best, brightly coloured activewear, insisting that we should try to 'look cute, but not too cute' for the content she's going to capture today. She appointed herself in charge of my new business Instagram (which doesn't yet exist), insisting she could get some good content to show the story of how my studio comes to be. It's a good idea and I'm grateful she thought of it, but her face matches what I'm thinking. This dump is never going to be anything worth filming.

"Come on Meg, I thought renovations were your thing," Rachel mocks, jumping over a broken chair and disappearing along the hallway.

"It smells like asshole in here," Meg scoffs, covering her mouth.

"You haven't eaten asshole if you think this is what it smells like," I reply.

Meg glares at me, her mouth parting in surprise. "You're right, I haven't eaten asshole."

"That makes two of us," Hazel adds.

"Prudes."

A delighted squeal comes from Rachel's direction at the back of the room. "I punched a hole in this wall!"

"Punch away!" I call out. "We're tearing them all down."

I hand a hammer to Meg and smile. "The sooner we knock this shit down, the sooner we can turn this into an oasis for the mind and body and less about asshole."

Meg gingerly takes the tool from me, her hand still covering her mouth. I fish out a mask from my kit and hand it to her. "Put this on. It'll help prevent the asbestos from getting in your lungs."

Meg's eyes widen and I can't contain my laugh. "I'm joking. It'll help with the smell. It's about to be a construction site in here, and I don't need you coughing your lungs up and ruining the day with a trip to the emergency room."

Meg snatches the mask from me and whips it on over her face. "Why are you in my life?"

Before waiting for a response, she edges her way in Rachel's direction. I hear Rachel shout a few seconds later and Meg screams, before cursing with a shriek.

"She's going to last about twenty minutes," Hazel muses, pulling on a pair of old gardening gloves.

"Ten," I reply, handing Hazel a mask. "Thank you for being here today. As you can see from this shitshow, I am in way over my head."

Hazel smiles, pulling her mask on. "I am so excited for you. Let's knock some shit down."

"Who knew how therapeutic smashing walls could be?" Hazel asks, as she collapses on a camping chair. She chugs from her water bottle before handing it to me.

Rachel nods as she wipes sweat from her brow. "I might quit my job and go into demolition."

I scull a few mouthfuls of water before looking at the disaster site in front of me. All the flimsy, temporary walls have now been smashed to smithereens, a mountain of debris covering the entire floor. I can now see the three brick walls which make up the space, but the amount of crap on the floor makes me think we're going to need help to get it out.

"I'm going to need to hire a few containers to get rid of all this junk," I murmur.

"Let me see if I can find a company." Meg taps at her phone. She's been sitting outside in another one of the camping chairs for the past hour, editing the content she filmed when we first got here. As we suspected, she wasn't keen to get her hands dirty and complained about the amount of dust, but she got some great footage of us tearing the place apart.

A low rumble turns all four of our heads to the carpark behind her and my stomach somersaults. The now familiar black truck of Anthony Bonetti trundles to a stop across the lot.

"Did you know he was coming?" Hazel asks me.

I shake my head.

The four of us watch as Anthony hops out from the driver's side, wearing a tight-fitted grey t-shirt and what appears to be the only type of shorts he owns—tradesmen shorts. Tight-fitting, black cargo shorts that make his butt look like a goddamned peach. He's donned his steel-cap work boots, making his calves look massive.

Rachel makes a purring sound under her breath. "Sweet Jesus, Kali. You're trying to resist *that*?"

I spent the better part of the morning updating the girls on my sexual tension and fantasies of one particular Bonetti brother.

"I know," I sigh, watching as Anthony rounds to the back of his tray, his corded muscles flexing in the sunlight.

Meg whips her head to me. "You made a bet to *not* touch him? *Look* at him. *Look* at the tattoos on his neck. *Look* at the *veins* in his neck." Meg fans the paper in her hand across her face, her eyes trained on the tattooed Adonis standing outside my shopfront.

Anthony turns and locks eyes with me and I forget to breathe. It's not until I register Meg filming my face that I snap out of my trance.

"Knock it off," I hiss at her, snatching her phone out of her hand.

She squeals and jumps out of her seat, taking it back. "This is movie gold. A love story and a new business venture. What more could the people want?"

"It's not a love story, so don't even think about trying to make it into one," I sneer.

Meg raises her perfectly raised eyebrows. "I *never* saw you look at my cousin like that and you were really into him."

"Alright, enough shit-stirring," Rachel says, steering Meg back inside. "Get onto that company so we can start clearing up this mess. But seriously, Kali. You look like your heart stopped beating."

Hazel bites back a grin as they head back inside, and I scowl at her. "Shut up."

"I didn't say anything," she says, waving to Anthony. "He hasn't stopped staring at you since he got here."

I glance back at Anthony and sure enough, his eyes are still on me, a blazing heat in them that sends a volt of pleasure to my toes.

"You gonna stare at me all day, Red?"

I roll my eyes as I start towards him. "Oh, spare me! I've got three witnesses who say you haven't taken your eyes off me since you pulled up."

When I stop in front of him, lust-filled eyes meet mine. "Busted. I could stare at you all day."

His words catch me by surprise, but Anthony doesn't give me time to respond. He presses a toolbox to my chest, and I fumble to hold the weight before he lets go. He reaches back into the tray and heaves a giant power tool into his arms, securing it between his hands and shoulder. "Let's get to work, Red."

"Get to work?"

"I'm good with my hands, remember?" he says waggling his eyebrows like some cartoon lech.

He swaggers ahead of me with ease and coolness, greeting Hazel like they've been best friends forever.

How the hell am I going to get any work done with this amount of electricity firing through my body? Not to mention, *knowing* the two of us are in on some stupid bet makes everything that much more heightened.

"You need a hand with that?"

I snap out of my gawking to see a kind smile sparkling in the sunlight. The man's feathered blonde hair blows in the breeze as he watches me expectantly. "I'm good thanks."

"Sorry if I startled you. I'm Nathan." He gestures behind him. "I run the pool supplies shop a few storefronts down."

"Pleasure," I reply. "I'm Kali and I'd shake your hand, but they're kind of full."

"I can see that." He turns to survey my bomb site shopfront. "Looks like a lot of impressive work going on there. A whole team of people getting it done."

"It's slave labour," I admit. "All they're getting is a pat on the back after this is over. I'm a terrible friend."

Nathan chuckles. "It was the same when I started my shop. That's what friends are for, right?"

"Damn straight."

Nathan grins and I don't miss the quick dart of his gaze down my body. "What business is this going to be?"

"A Pilates studio." I look at the construction site. "I can't see it yet, but my friends are cautiously optimistic."

"I'll have to hit you up for a discounted membership," Nathan jokes.

"Absolutely. I'd love more men in my classes. Especially handsome ones."

Nathan smirks. "Even if I'd be absolutely terrible?"

"You wouldn't be terrible," I assure him. "I'd help you. Pilates is for everybody, no matter your fitness level or flexibility."

"I'll remind you of that when I pull a muscle and can't walk for three days."

I laugh. "Deal."

Nathan draws his bottom lip between his teeth before exhaling deliberately. "Look, I'm not usually this forward, but you seem nice and easy to talk to and you're absolutely stunning. Would you like to go to dinner with me some time?"

I should've seen that coming. Flirting is so fun, I do it without thinking. I called him handsome and offered to help him in the space of two seconds. And he *is* handsome. He's charming and confident without being cocky. He runs his own business. He can hold a conversation.

Why aren't I jumping at the bit to accept a date with him?

"Oi, Kali!"

I whip my head to see Anthony standing in the entry. "You done flirting, or should we assume you're out for the day?"

I narrow my eyes at him and notice that whilst his tone had a humorous twang to it, his body is stiff, tension rolling off his shoulders.

"Is he your boyfriend?" Nathan's tone is laced with uncertainty as he looks at Anthony.

I scoff. "He wishes."

"Right. Well, you don't have to answer me right now about dinner—"

"I'd love to do dinner," I cut in.

"Great." Relief flitters across his face. "How about next Friday?"

Through my peripherals I see Anthony still watching our exchange. My heart rate picks up.

"Sounds great," I say with a smile. "I'll see you then."

He nods with a big smile and heads back towards his shop.

I adjust the toolbox in my arms and head back towards the warehouse. Anthony's still staring me down, his expression unreadable.

"What?" I snap, shoving the toolbox into his arms.

"Glad you could join us, Kali."

I push past him towards the girls inside, ignoring his searing gaze and the intoxicating sensation trickling through my veins at hearing *Kali* off his lips, instead of Red.

10

KALI

THE SETTING SUN over the distant mountains signals the end of the workday for most people. As we edge closer to winter, the days are getting shorter and the air cooler. We've put in a solid day of work and despite my jokes earlier about my friends working for free, I can't help but feel humbled by their help. Between the five of us, we managed to tear down every remaining wall and clear out half of the crap in there. The lot's dumpster is almost at capacity and until my one arrives tomorrow (thanks to Meg), I can't clear out anymore.

We all chatted amongst ourselves when we had bursts of energy, although Anthony had been quiet. But it was a *loud* quiet. He and I only exchanged a few words, almost as if he was pissed with me.

As I round the corner towards the dumpster, to squeeze one last bit of rubbish inside it, I'm yanked sideways by my waist. The rubbish in my hands falls to the ground as my back smacks against a brick wall, an enormous frame towering over me. Breathless, I gather my bearings and stare up into a pair of cobalt eyes filled with molten heat.

Anthony's face is inches from mine, his breath warm on my mouth. My heart beats out of my chest like a drum, and I wonder if it's possible for it to burst through flesh.

"What are you doing?" I gasp.

"I could ask you the same question," he growls. Anthony's gaze travels across my face and down my neck, electrifying my skin.

"I'm sorry. Are you braindead? You've bailed *me* against the wall like a psychopath."

Anthony frowns. "Are you seriously going on a date with that guy?"

My mouth opens and closes. I had not been expecting that and I'm torn between wanting the upper hand in our stupid game and wanting to succumb to his questions.

"I don't know what you're talking about."

Anthony's nostrils flare and he slides one of his large hands up my neck, enclosing it with his fingers on a gentle squeeze. I grin and gasp at the same time.

"Oh, you don't know what I'm talking about?" His lips trail down to my collarbone, the grip on my neck softening. "I have half a mind to take you right here in the carpark."

My chest heaves, no matter how hard I try to control it. "Are you an exhibitionist?"

Anthony chuckles. "There's a time and a place for it."

Visions of Anthony shoving my tights down and taking me right here, where anyone could see, flash through my mind, and my thighs clench.

"Let's get something straight," I force out. "I might be a woman who likes sex, but you're dreaming if you think I'm going to give it to you in plain sight."

"And I might be a man who *loves* sex, but that doesn't mean I'm going to take you outdoors for everyone to see."

"Really? Is that why you've bailed me up against this wall with talk of exhibitionism?"

"It's all part of my catalogue of moves, Red. Surely you know that."

Anthony leans back to peer down at me, the challenge evident on his face. He removes his hand from my neck and slides his thumb over my chin, tilting my head back ever-so-slightly.

Kiss me, kiss me, KISS ME.

A mischievous smirk spreads across Anthony's mouth as he lowers his face to mine. "Thinking about caving, Red?"

"Not even slightly, Bonetti."

He presses his hips to mine, and my mouth drops open on a sigh at his hardness. "I'd say you're dangerously close to conceding there," I whisper, embarrassed by the shake in my tone.

Anthony continues his soft, but deadly assault of gentle kisses up the other side of my neck. "If you check the rules ma'am, we agreed that a kiss on the lips sealed the deal."

"That's one hell of a loophole," I pant.

"You only have yourself to blame."

He rolls his hips again and a whimper escapes my mouth. Anthony tenses at the sound and he reaches around to grip the back of my neck.

His muscular chest crushes against my breasts. My fingers grip the fabric of his shirt, fisting it into my hands as he grinds against me again and again. Heat builds below my stomach; my breaths growing more rampant. He leans back to look at me, his mouth parted as he watches my pleasure build.

"Kali! I've got the dumpster guys on the phone. *Kali!*"

Meg's annoyed screeches break me out of my trance, and I push against Anthony's body, his eyes blinking as though he's caught in the same haze as me.

"I've gotta go," I croak, shoving his shoulder as I push past him. "Pick up that rubbish!"

I don't miss the way he smirks at my frazzled demeanour or how he unashamedly adjusts his crotch.

Lord, help me.

11

ANTHONY

THE LASER-CUT machine comes to a halt, and I shut it off, removing the plank of wood from the table. Every time I use this thing, I'm impressed with its accuracy. I know technology means you can't really mess this up, but it still blows me away what a template in one of these machines can do. If you have your settings right, it'll cut out whatever you want.

In this case, a mandala. It's a new one for me and one of the most complex templates I've ever created. The machine might do all the hard work, but it's going to take a lot of patience from me to put the pieces together. A lot of checking and re-checking before I even think about getting the glue out. Especially because I keep getting distracted.

Kali's lust-filled gaze, the sound of her pants, the way she'd gripped my shirt and pulled me closer. I've taken the memory of me pushing her up against that wall and cut it down into bite-sized moments, replaying them over and over so they're now branded in my mind.

Blood rushes to my dick as I remember how Kali's hips moved against mine. She wanted it as badly as I did. I wonder if one of us would've caved if we'd been alone. I take a deep breath, willing my junk to behave itself, but it's useless. My junk is almost bursting through the fabric of my pants at mere memories.

"Looks good." Patrick abruptly appears at my side, peering at the sheets of timber, all with different patterns and cut-outs.

"My hard-on or the artwork?"

Patrick's gaze darts to my crotch before offering a disgruntled scoff. "Jesus, Anthony. Please tell me you're not so egotistical that you're getting off on your own work."

I grin and turn away from him, shoving my hand in my boxers to adjust myself. "Not quite. You can blame Kali Cooper for this."

"Did something happen between you two?"

"Not exactly." I glance over my shoulder at my brother, who's leaning against the wall with his arms folded. "Barely anything."

"Barely anything, but enough for you to be wanking off in your art studio?"

"I wasn't wanking," I reply, turning back to face him. "I was thinking."

"You were thinking about Kali and got a hard-on?" Patrick clarifies. "You're in trouble."

"Maybe, but I'm not mad about it."

Patrick nods. "I figured as much. Whatever you two are playing at, promise me you'll be smart about it."

"You are such a dad," I sigh.

Patrick's brow furrows. "You're not the first person to tell me that."

"I'm not going to do anything stupid."

"I know you're not." Patrick straightens up from the wall. "I'm just saying that you're my brother and Kali is Hazel's best friend—"

"And you're worried I'm going to fuck it up." My heavy words hang in the air between us. We both know that my calling card in life has been to screw things up. I wonder how often he believes in the good in me or if he secretly wonders when I'll break down and ruin everything for him again.

"That is *not* what I meant." Patrick's voice is cold steel as he glares at me. "I meant it's a small circle and things have the potential to get messy. I want you to protect *yourself*, Anthony. Your wellbeing is all I care about."

I roll my eyes. "Yeah, yeah. Don't spiral out of control and ruin our lives again."

Patrick steps forward, closing the gap between us swiftly. "I don't think that about you, and I don't want you thinking that about yourself either," Patrick orders. "You have made tremendous progress and showed remarkable restraint. I trust you implicitly. Understood?"

Patrick's eyes are heated with promise as he stares me down and I can't help but falter. He's stopped doing our regular check-ins. He doesn't demand to know where I'm going or when I'm coming home anymore. I believe he trusts me.

"Okay, okay," I say, shoving him lightly in the shoulder. "I hear you loud and clear, *dad*."

Patrick steps back and visibly exhales, his gaze falling back to the mandala art piece. "This piece is going to be beautiful."

I stand back to take in what I've done so far, and it only reaffirms my initial assumption. Gluing these pieces together is going to take a shitload of time. "Thanks."

"Is it a new design?"

"Yep." I wipe dust off my hands with a rag as I step back. "Haven't figured out how it's all going to come together yet, but I'll get there."

Patrick's eyes narrow, his gaze trailing over the swirls and lines of the wood I've cut and moulded. Not much rattles me these days, but his curious eyes seeing new pieces of art for the first time always sends heat up my neck. "Beautiful. Is it for anyone in particular?"

"Nah, just keeping my hands busy."

The words roll off my tongue so effortlessly, I almost believe them.

Patrick nods, seemingly satisfied with my answer and turns to leave the workshop. "Maria's bringing paella over in an hour. Will you be joining us?"

"For paella? Hell yes."

"Great. When she asks you who you're making this piece for, make sure you double down on your lying face. That was an abysmal effort." Patrick walks out the door without looking back.

He knows me too well.

12

KALI

EVERYTHING ACHES.

As someone who's been fit and healthy for most of her life, I can say with confidence I've awoken muscles I've never used before. My back, butt and arms pulsate with a pain akin to that of my early dancing days.

I've almost stripped the entire space of the old junk. From six o'clock this morning to now, twelve hours later, I've pulled up dirty carpet, coughed on dust, dragged random bits of metal across the room and scrubbed stains off walls. Whilst I'm channelling independent badass woman, I hate that it looks like I've barely made a dent.

My stomach rumbles, a sign I should get some sustenance in me if I want to keep working into the night. I eye the granola bar next to my bag and screw my nose up with a sigh. It'll have to do. If I leave to get food, there's no way I'll come back. I'll sink into a chair and fall asleep.

My phone buzzes and I swipe to answer. "Hey."

"How's it going up there?" Hazel asks.

"Good. Except, I'm starving, sore and may or may not be panicking that I've bitten off more than I can chew."

Hazel laughs. "If anyone can do this, you can. I promise I can come and help tomorrow, and you can put me to work."

"Thanks, Hazy. I don't think I'll be back for wine and pizza tonight. We're going to have to hold off on the new doco."

Hazel groans. "Need I remind you they have footage of this psycho *helping* in the search for the victims?"

"I know, I know. We'll watch it this weekend. Promise."

"You're lucky I'm a forgiving person," she huffs. "How much more do you think you'll do tonight?"

"I want to try to undo the old light fixtures, but I'm pretty sure I need a ladder and some sort of manly tool." Those little buggers are rusted on for sure.

A muffled voice comes through the speaker, but I can't make out the words. "Did you say something?"

"Anthony says he's got a manly tool that can help. He'll bring it over."

"Anthony's there?"

"Yeah, he's working on the desk."

"And you have me on speaker without giving me warning? What if I opened with a fact about my vagina?" I snap.

"I'm always on speaker these days, Kali, while I'm drawing. And Anthony would love any fact about your vagina."

"Tell him not to come here."

"He already left. I've never seen him move so fast."

I groan, ignoring my brain telling me not to sit down and sink into a camping chair.

"What's up with you?" Hazel asks. "Do you have blue balls? Wait, it'd be called something else, wouldn't it?"

"Pretty sure it's blue bean."

"Blue bean? That's revolting."

"Yet, perfectly accurate."

Hazel hums her agreement. "So, you've got a blue bean?"

"I do," I groan. "And my self-control is dwindling at a pathetic rate."

"What happens if you lose again?"

I remind Hazel of the rules of the agreement I'm determined not to lose, particularly because if I do, I have to go on a date with a man I'm enjoying toying with.

Hazel snorts. "We all know where this is going; building up all that sexual tension until you can rip each other's clothes off."

"Well, obviously," I sigh. "But I'm not going to be the first to break."

"Your competitive and passionate nature stops you from experiencing joy." Hazel chuckles, knowing that the line my grandmother uses on me will rile me up.

"I'm the most joyful person I know."

"You *are* very joyful," Hazel agrees. "However, you're purposely depriving yourself of hot sex and therefore, becoming very *un*-joyful. Who cares if you lose? You'll have great sex and be wined and dined by a beautiful man."

"Who cares if I lose? Do you know me at all?"

"I know you hate losing, but I also know you enjoy penis," Hazel says. "And I'm pretty sure you were the one who told me to get some penis in my life to be happy."

"And I stand by that. Just not Bonetti penis."

Hazel clucks. "I wouldn't write it off, *trust me*."

"I don't even know you anymore."

"Bye blue bean," Hazel sings.

After we hang up, I allow myself to sink into the chair, images of a sweaty Anthony Bonetti flashing through my brain. I don't even try to fight it, which is stupid, because the ache between my legs starts almost immediately.

Movement in my peripheral vision snaps me out of my daydream and I leap out of the chair. My stance is pure Jackie Chan, feet apart planted firmly to the floor, right hand lifted. There's nobody there, but there's a piece of paper sticky-taped to the wall near the entrance that wasn't there before.

I edge my way across the room to the open roller door, peering out in the empty carpark. My car is the only one here. When I glance at the paper my eyes widen.

WATCH YOUR BACK, SLUT.

The sound of snickering reaches my ears and I duck my head around the corner to see teenagers on bikes at the other end of the lot. A chill runs through my body before the anger kicks in. I march outside into the brisk air and watch as they try to peddle away.

"Is this the best you could do?" I call out after them. "Dickheads!"

I hear them laughing as they disappear into the darkness, and I stomp back inside.

It doesn't take a genius to figure out why those kids are pissed with me. Patrick pointed out that this warehouse used to be a hangout for miscreant teens and squatters who got high before I moved in.

"Give me strength," I hiss under my breath. I toss the paper onto my makeshift desk, opting to conserve the little energy I have left instead of chasing down those deadbeats like a mad woman.

13

KALI

THE GRAVEL on the driveway crunches and I see Anthony's enormous black truck pull up outside. He jumps out of the cab with the agility of an athlete, slamming the door behind him with ease. His grey singlet has the sides cut out, exposing the ink on his ribs. The patterns contort as he swaggers to the tray of his truck.

I'm salivating.

"I heard you need a manly tool." Anthony saunters up to the open door, letting out a whistle as he takes in the space. "Shit, Red. Look at this place. It's a whole new room."

"I can't tell whether you're being truthful or sarcastic right now."

Anthony smiles as he places his toolbox on the floor. "It looks great."

"Is that why you raced here to rescue me?"

He rolls his eyes. "I'm *helping*, not rescuing. You don't need to turn down help. Let me grab my ladder."

I watch him as he retrieves his ladder, definitely not focusing on the way the muscles in his lean arms contort under the weight.

When Anthony reaches me, he holds his hand out and hands me a small parcel. "I thought you might be hungry."

"That's for me?" My mouth waters at the brick of foil in his hand.

"Yeah. A vegetarian burrito. It's got jackfruit or some shit in it."

"Oh, thank you!" I cry, snatching it up and tearing the top open.

Anthony laughs as he places his ladder on the concrete floor. "Jonesy said food would soften the blow, but I didn't think it'd make you this happy."

I'm certain my eyes roll into the back of my head as I bite into the wrap, my tastebuds dancing with delight as the flavour hits my tongue. "Oh my god, thank you," I moan. "You don't happen to have a beer in that magical toolbox, do you?"

Anthony looks amused as he quirks an eyebrow, but he doesn't answer me. "Where's the shit you want off the walls?"

I wave lazily to the far wall. "I don't know what they are, but they're not moving."

Anthony climbs his ladder with practised ease, his strong thighs and work boots holding him in place as he casually leans across to jimmy the light fixtures. "Yeah, they're rusted on. I should be able to get them off though."

"You think so?"

"I can get anything off." Anthony doesn't even look at me as he climbs down the ladder, grinning at his own joke.

"You never stop, do you?"

"Never."

For the next fifteen minutes, I unashamedly sit in the camping chair, finishing my burrito and watching Anthony's sinewy arms contract as he works his skills on the stubborn fixtures. He gets the rusted items off the walls with ease and wanders back to me when he's finished.

"Did you enjoy the show?" he asks, a smirk playing on his mouth.

I smile, unabashed. "Oh, yes. I'm sad it's over."

"It doesn't have to be." Anthony's growl elicits a shiver up the back of my neck that's almost painful, like his words are fire against my flesh. He drops the items onto the desk and his expression glimmers from predatory to concerned in a matter of seconds.

"What's this?"

I glance at the piece of paper under Anthony's hand. "It's nothing. Stupid kids playing pranks."

Anthony frowns. "Doesn't sound like a prank so much as a threat. Who are these kids?"

"I saw a few of them on their bikes laughing before you got here. They weren't menacing in any way, only stupid teenagers picking on the hot new chick." I throw him an exaggerated wink, but he doesn't relent.

"Kali, you should report this."

"Report that a bunch of teens are trying to scare me away after I took ownership of where they used to hang out and get high?" I offer. "I'm not worried. They'll find somewhere else to shoot up."

Anthony clenches his jaw and nods. "Yeah, they will."

He tosses the paper out of his fingers and returns to his tools by the ladder. To my surprise he collects his items and collapses the ladder with a resounding crash, scooping down to wedge it under his arm, his toolbox in his hands.

"You're leaving?" Unexpected disappointment floods through me.

"Yep. Night." He marches past me without another word. I watch as he throws his items into the back of his truck carelessly, the bangs ricocheting into the night sky. He peels out of the carpark before I've even processed what happened.

What did I say?

14

ANTHONY

I ACTED like a dick the other night. A first class, grade-A dick.

I've got years of group therapy and one-on-one sessions with Angela up my sleeve. I've had countless conversations with friends and strangers about drugs and alcohol. And yet, all it took was one comment from Kali about kids getting high and I lost my temper.

I couldn't help it. My teeth ground together as tunnel vision took over. Memories of getting high for countless years raged through my brain. Hanging out with the wrong people, the grief I gave my family who were only trying to help. Years and years wasted as I blamed everybody else for my failures. Remembering the moment with Chloe that changed everything. It's been almost four years, but sometimes, it feels like four minutes.

My life is a constant battle of figuring out how the hell to be a sober, functioning person. Some days I do so well, I think nothing could ever break me. Other days, like that night with Kali, I freak and spiral out of control.

When it comes to that woman, I don't know what I'm doing.

Ma always said I was an angry kid, but I never believed her

until it got me in serious trouble. Punching walls when I got into arguments I couldn't win, kicking shoes left on the floor when I wasn't allowed something. It took a long time and a lot of heartache for my parents before I got that shit handled.

I switch off the laser machine and step back from my workstation. This is pointless. I'm going to mess up every piece of wood I have if I keep working while angry.

"Bad day?"

I turn to face my brother, who's leaning against the doorframe. "Bad week."

"What happened?"

I blow out a dramatic breath. "Kali doesn't know about me. About Chloe."

Patrick's expression doesn't falter, but I notice his folded arms tense. Considering I've mentioned the former love of his life who died because of me, he's remarkably calm.

"I haven't told her about any of it," I continue. "About who I used to be and what I used to do. She doesn't know I'm sober and going to meetings. I haven't told her what happened ... none of it."

"And you're worried about what her reaction might be." It's a statement, not a question.

I shrug. "Must be. Every time I think I'm going to tell her, I pussy out."

"That's not like you."

"No shit." I run a hand over my head in annoyance. "She made some comment about kids getting high the other day and instead of telling her about me, I got pissed and walked off."

Patrick shakes his head. "You removed yourself from a situation instead of blowing up. Sounds like a victory to me."

I sigh. "I don't get it. I told Jonesy without a second thought."

"You told Hazel in an attempt to clear *my* name." Patrick

wanders so he's standing closer to me. "This is different. You clearly like Kali."

I groan. "Don't start."

"You know I'm right."

I'm not getting into that with my brother today.

"Some kids left some threatening words on a note on her door," I tell him, deflecting. "It might be nothing, but could you check it out?"

Patrick nods with a frown. "Of course."

My phone buzzes and I glance down. It's Kali. Patty's gaze burns a hole in the side of my face. I click my phone shut and slip it back into my pocket.

"I might not be an expert with women," Patrick says. "But ignoring them only makes it worse."

"I'll keep that in mind."

15

KALI

WITH THE VIOLENCE of a woman scorned, I slam my car door shut.

Hazel looks at me, alarmed. "Kali! You're going to break something if you don't chill out."

"I'm fine."

I am *not* fine. Ever since Anthony stormed out of my studio a week ago, I've been uncontrollably angry and moody. We haven't spoken since. I've sent him several texts and even attempted a phone call. No response. He hasn't come around to work on the desk for Hazel and hasn't dropped by the studio.

I've gone over our last interaction a hundred times, and it makes me furious. We talked about light fixtures, burritos and the empty threat I got from a bunch of teenagers. Whatever I said to piss him off isn't clear to me. I would apologise if I knew what the hell to apologise for. And now, *my* moodiness and anger are building and building because he's forgotten how to use a phone.

I unlock the roller door and push it open, and Hazel and I head inside. Hazel flicks on the lights, frowning at the space in front of her.

"I know. There's still a shitload to do."

Hazel smiles. "But it's getting there. I'm proud of you."

Ordinarily, those sorts of words would lift my spirits, but I'm too annoyed at a certain tattooed man to concentrate. I'm also annoyed at myself for allowing a man to take up so much real estate in my head. When was the last time I cared this much?

"I've got to see if I can borrow a ladder to finish painting around the trims up there." Now that the air con fixtures are in, I can get to work painting the walls and turning this into something useable, rather than a worksite. I glance down at my phone and inspect the to-do list unravelling before my eyes.

"Isn't Anthony painting the trims?" Hazel asks.

"I don't think Anthony will come back, somehow," I say with a snort.

"Anthony's just having a bad time. He'll come back around."

I scoff. "I don't know how you can be so forgiving of his mood swings."

"Practice," she says dryly.

"Good point. I've got enough trouble keeping mine under control, so I don't need his on top of that. I'll be happy if I never see him again."

Hazel raises her eyebrows, pursing her lips as she looks over my shoulder. "Well, this should be interesting."

I spin to see Patrick and Anthony getting out of their cars outside. My stomach flutters with anticipation, battling against anger and confusion. Shame and embarrassment are also smugly present. I have no idea where I stand with this man.

The two men approach the front of the shop, Patrick leading the way. His face lights up when he sees Hazel and he gives me a courteous nod. My gaze flicks to his brother, whose face reveals nothing when he makes eye contact with me.

"Good morning," Patrick says, his eyes roaming the space. "Kali, it's looks great."

"Thanks. It's got a long way to go."

"What are you guys doing here?" Hazel asks, wrapping her arms around Patrick's waist. He closes his eyes as if he's breathing in her scent and kisses the top of her head.

"We thought we'd stop by to see how it's going, see if there's anything we can do to help," Patrick says with a smile.

"In your suit?" I ask.

"Hey, I can get my hands dirty."

"Thanks, but we've got it handled."

"You *would* say that," Anthony mutters, swaggering up.

My hands are on my hips, my nails digging into my skin. "No one asked you to come here, Bonetti. If you can't pull the stick out of your ass, feel free to leave."

He rolls his eyes. "Yeah, I'm the one with the stick up my ass."

"You were the one who left last week. Have you got something to say?"

Anthony steps forward. "You know it. How much time have you got?"

"Oookay." Hazel steps between us and offers me a gritted smile. She places her hands on my shoulders and steers me backwards. "Let's take a breath, shall we?"

I inhale deeply, before exhaling through my nostrils.

"I wanted to come down and check the place out," Patrick explains. "Anthony said you got a threat?"

"For God's sake, it's nothing." I stare daggers at Anthony, but he stares right back, unrelenting.

"You know, I can appreciate your strong will and go-getter attitude most days," Anthony says. "But I never thought you'd be so stupid when it comes to your own safety."

"Well luckily no one here is asking for your opinion."

"I swear to God—"

"One more word Bonetti! One more *fucking* word—"

"Alright, enough!" Patrick cuts in, throwing his hands in the air. He tilts his head to look at Hazel, who's eyes are wide, and her mouth slammed shut as if she's battling a smile. "Jesus, it's like dealing with teenagers."

"I'm ready to let them have it out." Hazel shrugs. "Kali did say you were a bit like a dad. It's kind of true."

Patrick ignores her. "Kali, I'm a former detective."

"Thank you for the reminder about how you lied to us for months on end," I snap.

"Let me at least do some basics?" he asks. "Install some cameras and a decent alarm. Maybe do a poke around of who your neighbours are?"

"That's not basic. That's an invasion of privacy."

Anthony throws his hands up. "It's *smart!*"

"Zip it." Hazel shoots Anthony a warning look, who huffs and folds his arms.

"Please Kali," Patrick says, his frown creased with concern.

"I'll allow the cameras and the alarm. But please leave my neighbours out of this for now. Things are stressful enough without adding any extra drama."

Patrick nods in appreciation and heads out the door to look at the front entrance, his figurative policeman hat on as he walks up and down scoping out the area.

I glare at Anthony. "I don't know when you appointed yourself as someone who needs to get involved in my life, but you are hereby dismissed from that responsibility."

"I'm not going *anywhere*," he hisses.

"But I am," Hazel singsongs, following Patrick outside.

I take a step towards Anthony. "I am a grown woman who's been to hell and back in my lifetime. I managed fine without you then; I can manage without you now."

Anthony drops his arms and takes a step, closing the space between us. "You're so fixated on keeping everyone out, you can't see when someone is genuinely trying to help. Get over yourself."

"I have never met someone I want to strangle more in my entire life," I bite.

Anthony's mouth curves into a smirk. "You've thought about that haven't you, Red? Your fingers curved around my throat, pressing hard into my skin as I bring you to orgasm again and again?"

A strangled noise escapes my throat, but no words come out. The surprise must be evident on my face, because Anthony's smirk morphs into a smug grin. He leans down until I can feel his breath just above my ear. "Knew it," he rasps.

My breaths become shallow at the sudden change in the atmosphere. It's unpredictable. Stark coldness to fiery, heated passion which sucks oxygen out of my lungs.

"I'm not going anywhere," he repeats. Despite the rage coursing through my vein's, his insistence on sticking around doesn't annoy me. It brings me comfort.

"You're going to insist on being a pain in my ass, aren't you?" I whisper. "Take the hint, Bonetti. I don't need anyone rescuing me or protecting me."

He narrows his eyes at me, assessing. "Why are you fighting this?"

"What?"

"I mean, at first, I thought it was funny and you were messing with me as much as I'm messing with you, but ... you're *really* fighting this."

Anthony peers down at me, the blue in his eyes darkening. He's so close to me I can smell his minty breath. "What are you so afraid of?"

My mouth opens and closes, and a strangled chortling sound comes from the back of my throat. But that's about as far as I get.

"I'm not afraid of anything," I croak out.

"Your lies don't fool me, Red." Anthony's gaze darts to my mouth. It would be so easy to reach up and kiss him.

"Sorry, am I interrupting something?" Nathan stands in the large entrance, sweeping his gaze between the two of us.

The word *no* shrills from my mouth right as Anthony growls *yes*. We look at each other again and Anthony's nostrils flare.

I give Nathan my brightest smile. "Not at all, Nathan. How can I help?"

"I wanted to … confirm tonight with you." He flashes a smug smile at Anthony.

My stomach drops. The date. I'd forgotten all about it. After the way Anthony had bailed me against the wall and brought me food when he came to help, I had every intention of cancelling. But it completely slipped my mind after Anthony stormed out of here last weekend.

"We're definitely still on," I reply.

Tension rolls off Anthony in thick waves. He cracks his knuckles by squeezing his fists together and I look at him, momentarily guilt-ridden at the fleeting look of vulnerability on his face.

"Let me give you guys some privacy," Anthony growls, as he rolls his broad shoulders back and walks past Nathan, distaste evident on his face.

"Don't mind him, he's got the emotional intelligence of a twelve-year-old," I dismiss. As the words leave my mouth, I wish I could suck them back in.

Nathan chortles. "Understood. The dinner reservation is for seven. Should I pick you up at six-thirty? Gives us time for a drink beforehand."

"Sure. I'll text you my address."

Nathan beams at me. "Great. Can't wait."

"Me too."

The words sound empty in my ears, but Nathan seems pleased as he smiles down at me.

Your lies don't fool me, Red.

I don't think they're fooling me either.

16

KALI

NATHAN IS HANDSOME, with that pretty boy-next-door look going on. Soft blonde hair and sparkling blue eyes that twinkle when I laugh at his jokes. He's a naturally, charismatic storyteller and he's been doing his best to make me laugh and capture my attention since we got here, but I'm not interested. Is this what happens when you start a business? You don't have the energy or care to date?

I can bullshit my way in or out of anything and I'm doing it now. My lack of interest has nothing to do with the fact that I'm setting up my own business. It's because I can't get that sexy, tattooed menace out of my brain for longer than a minute.

When Anthony told me to enjoy my date, it brought me a split-second of satisfaction, replaced by guilt, regret and the overwhelming sensation of wanting to cancel. If he had just answered his stupid phone, none of this would have escalated and I would've turned Nathan down. *Goddamned Bonetti.*

"How's the studio coming along? Looks like you've made some solid headway with it." Nathan's smile is hopeful, probably praying I give him something more substantial than a hair toss and nod.

"It's going great," I reply, straightening my shoulders. "It's a lot of hard work, but I'm loving it, because it's *my* hard work. Even though it's stressful as all hell."

Nathan nods. "Opening your own business can really test you as a human being."

I chuckle. "It sure can."

I wonder what Nathan would look like with a shaved head and tattoos. Would he look as good as Ant—

"Have you had any issues with teenagers at your shop?" I ask quickly.

Nathan tilts his head in thought. "You mean the three musketeers who are always loitering around on their bikes?"

"That'd be them."

Nathan shakes his head. "Never had any problems. Although to be fair, they used to keep to themselves in your warehouse before the landlord put the padlock on."

I sigh. "Yeah, I gathered that much. They're not too happy I've taken over their hangout. They left a not-so-friendly note the other day."

Nathan looks thoughtful. "They strike me as the types that'd leave you alone for a small fee."

"You mean, pay them to leave me alone?" I ask. "That's opening a can of worms."

"They're deadbeat teenagers. They'll do anything for a quick buck."

Instinctively, I scrunch up my nose at his words. "I don't think I need to go down that route."

Nathan shrugs. "Fair enough. You want another drink?"

I glance at my half-full glass of wine. "I'm good."

"How about a margarita?" he cuts in, wiggling his eyebrows. "Something tells me you're a spicy marg kind of woman."

I laugh. "You got me."

Nathan waves to the nearest server and I lean back in my chair, watching as he orders us new drinks.

One margarita won't hurt.

For someone who considers herself a seasoned drinker, I somehow failed miserably tonight.

Halfway through my second cocktail, I felt stupidly drunk. Nathan and I got chatty, and I somehow ended up focusing more on our conversation than eating the food on our table. But still, I was surprised when the wooziness crept up on me.

Everything spins on the drive home, exhaustion threatening my eyelids the entire journey. I didn't realise how hard I'd been working lately until this moment.

Nathan realises he's left his laptop at his shop, so we stop by before he drops me home. "I'll just be a sec," he sings out as he hops out of the car.

I open the passenger door. "All good. I need some fresh air anyway." My feet land on the ground and suddenly everything tilts on an axis. I reach out and stumble against the side of the car. "Whoa."

Nathan rushes around to me, concern etched on his blurry face. "You feel alright?"

"Turns out I'm a lightweight these days," I mumble, using his arms to straighten myself up.

Nathan grins down at me. "Did you want to come inside for a bit? We could have a nightcap."

I shake my head. "No thanks. I've definitely had enough." My cheeks are warm, and my vision is spotty. I can't believe how quickly a bit of tequila knocked me over.

"Just one more?" he pleads.

"She said she's had enough." The words split my skin open; my veins pulsate. Anthony is standing mere feet away, watching us with furious eyes.

17

ANTHONY

I KNEW there was something off about this guy.

He's standing too close to Kali, her hands grasped around his arms. He's getting pushy about getting her more liquored up and I can tell by the glazed look on her face that she's had a few.

"She's a grown woman who can make her own decisions," Nathan snaps.

"And you're a grown man who should know better than to take advantage of an intoxicated woman," I spit.

Nathan glares at me. "That's not what's happening here."

"Sure, looks like it." I glance at Kali, whose eyes lock with mine. "You okay?"

"I'm fine," she mutters. "I can take care of myself."

"Sure, you can." I stifle an eye roll and turn to Nathan. "Time to call it a night."

"Time for you to mind your own business," he spits.

I step closer to them and Nathan releases Kali to meet me. Two seconds later, she's sliding against the car again, heading for the ground.

I leap forward, shoving Nathan out of the way and catching

Kali before she collapses on the gravel. She groans under her breath, tilting her head up to look at me. "Something feels wrong," she grumbles.

My blood simmers with rage as I take in her pained expression. I know exactly what she means. She can't stand up. She's dazed and confused. I want to drag this asshole around the back of the building and pummel him until I've got no skin left on my knuckles.

I gently lower Kali to the ground, making sure she's leaning against the car, before standing up to face Nathan. "How many drinks did she have tonight?"

Nathan shrugs. "A lot. We were having a good time."

Kali groans. "I had three."

My fists reach out and grab Nathan by the shirt, pulling him close to me. Panic flitters across his eyes. "You slipped her something."

Nathan scoffs. "Calm it down with the dramatics, mate. She's just drunk."

"Do you always liquor women up to the point of incoherence? Can't get it up unless they're incapacitated?"

Nathan grabs my fists and yanks himself free. "Fuck off."

I step closer to Nathan and smirk as he flinches backwards. "Get the fuck out of here before I *make* you get out of here."

Before my anger gets the better of me, I lean down and scoop Kali off the ground, her arms reaching up around my neck as we head back towards her studio. A few seconds later, I hear Nathan's car leave the lot.

"You had to get all macho, didn't you?" Kali mumbles from under me.

I walk us back inside and gently lower her into a camping chair. "You're welcome."

She peers up at me, her eyes narrowed. "What's your problem?"

"Have you forgotten the last few minutes? Kali, you're incapacitated. You had three drinks, and you can't even walk. There's no way he didn't have a hand in that."

Kali's eyes widen. "Nathan wouldn't do that. The tequila just went to my head."

"Yes, by all means, defend that piece of shit," I spit, handing her a bottle of water. "Drink this."

Kali's eyes flicker back and forth as she takes a few swigs, before focusing on the space around her, as if suddenly realising where she is. "What are you even doing here?"

"I finished painting the trims like I promised. I was finishing up the front counter when you and Romeo pulled up."

"You don't have better things to do on a Friday night?"

"Nope."

Kali stares at me. I want to know what she's thinking. Most of the time I can get a good read on her. Despite the heated dynamics between the two of us, she usually skips any game-playing and tells me what she thinks straight up. *Now?* I've no idea what's running through her mind, especially if she's not clear-headed.

"What?" she asks, and I realise I'm staring at her.

"Why did you go on that date tonight?"

Kali's eyes widen with surprise. She ducks her head and starts rummaging through her bag. "Because I wanted to."

"Why?"

She huffs, slowly standing from her chair. "Because he's cute and charming and *nice* to me. Well, I *thought* he was."

"I'm not nice?" I ask, stepping forward so she doesn't fall again. Her breathing escalates. It's hard to ignore how her body responds to mine.

"You're only nice to me when you're trying to get something from me," she mumbles.

"That's not true."

"No?" She lifts her chin. "So, you're not all up in my grill now to try to win this stupid bet?"

I tower over her. "I'm up in your grill because I *want* to be up in your grill."

Kali blinks several times before responding. "I don't get you."

"What's not to get? I've been nothing but transparent since the day I met you. And if you think the bet is stupid, let's call it off."

Kali narrows her eyes. "I'm no quitter."

"Then stop whinging."

Kali scoffs. "I'm not *whinging*. Stop projecting your mind games onto me. Take it up with your therapist."

I can't help but chuckle. "Why are you so fixated on the fact that I go to therapy?"

"I'm not. I used to go religiously."

"Why'd you stop?"

Kali hesitates. "Thirteen years of it was my limit."

Something in my chest loosens. "Maybe you should try again."

Kali hums to herself, her feisty demeanour replaced by one much softer, her arms wrapped around herself like a cocoon. "Maybe. Figure out why I self-sabotage all the time." Her voice drifts off, as if she's talking to herself.

"I could point you in the right direction," I offer. "Since moving here I've gathered all sorts of contacts. There's a good spread of mental health professionals around."

Kali's mouth twists in thought. "Maybe."

It's quiet for several beats, Kali staring down at the floor. She's not herself right now. If she has been drugged or even spiked with extra alcohol, she needs to get somewhere safe to sober up. Having this conversation when she's not in her right mind isn't fair, as much as I might want her to open up.

"Want me to take you home?" I ask.

Kali's eyes flash to mine, a heat behind them that wasn't there before. Like maybe she's had a moment of clarity or entered another realm of wasted. "No." She steps forward and palms the front of my shorts so unexpectedly, a choke hisses from my throat.

I grab her wrist to stop her. "Kali, you're not yourself right now."

"So?" She reaches up into the crook of my neck and gently bites my earlobe. My dick strains against the fabric encasing it.

I grab her shoulders and steer her back. "I just scared off a guy for taking advantage of you. I'm not about to do the same."

Kali pouts, running her hands over my chest. Her fingers trace over the curves beneath my t-shirt, lingering on the swirls of ink creeping up my neck. "I could lick you from head to toe," she murmurs.

I groan. "Jesus, Red."

Her brow scrunches as she rests her hands over my heart. "Your heart is racing."

"That happens a lot when I'm around you."

Her gaze meets mine and her playfulness vanishes. Her body tenses, her eyes searching, as if she's checking my eyes for any sign of deceit.

"What if he did slip me something?" she whispers, fear evident in her voice. "I had two cocktails and a glass of wine. Some of it's already a blur."

Pain spasms in my gums as I grind down on my teeth. *I'm going to kill that motherfucker.*

"Why did you say yes to a date with this guy, when you didn't want to?" I ask.

"I was going to cancel," she insists. "But you wouldn't text me back. You ignored me." She shrugs with one shoulder and a steam roller of guilt slams into me. "I don't know why I said yes in the first place. I do that a lot. I go on dates when I don't always want to."

"Why?"

"I don't know." She glances up at me with her big brown eyes. "I'm ... I guess I'm ..."

Any remnants of anger and jealousy dissipate as I watch her struggle to find the words to express herself. The way she's staring *into* me almost hurts. "I'm broken," she whispers.

"Kali ..." I reach for her hand on my chest and our fingers intertwine. "You're not broken."

"You only call me Kali when you're mad," she mumbles, staring at our hands. "Or when you're serious."

I want to stay in this bubble, with Kali's vulnerability, but it's not right that I'm asking her these questions and having this talk with her when she probably won't remember any of it tomorrow.

"Let's get you home," I mutter. "I'll lock up."

Disappointment flits across Kali's face and I wonder if she feels the energy between us snuff out like a light. She nods in agreement as I steer her into the camping chair.

I sensed the shift was happening before tonight, but now I'm certain. It's clear as day. I want to know everything she's thinking. I want to jump inside her skin and let her spill her secrets onto me. I want to connect on every level, every vulnerability, every thought.

I want to know more about Kali than I ever thought possible, and it's got nothing to do with the stupid bet.

18

KALI

A HOT-SEARING pain shoots through my skull and smacks me behind the eyeballs. A groan escapes my cotton-dry mouth as I force my eyelids open.

I'm in my room. *Thank God.*

I dare to peer to my left to see if anyone is next to me—empty. I can't see any clothing that's not mine strewn across the floor, but when my eyes snap to my bedside table, my heart sinks a little. A glass of untouched water and an empty aspirin packet sit there laughing at me.

"What an amateur," I groan, reaching for the glass. Last night is a splotchy blur. I only remember snippets of my date and the aftermath with Anthony. One thing I'm certain of is that I had zero filter last night.

Movement in the hallway makes me sit up and I clutch my head with a groan. Hazel is banging around like the goddamned elephant woman. She knows the rules. I need quiet before coffee—hangover or no.

I manage to get out of bed and cross the room, heading towards the noise to make my displeasure clear.

"Good morning!"

I grab my head as the pain rips through again, squinting at the man looming in my kitchen. "Bonetti, what the hell are you doing here?"

"That's no way to greet your house guests," he sings, spooning cereal into his mouth.

I straighten up, taking in his shirtless torso sprawled with ink, the way his defined v dips into his low-hanging track pants. If I wasn't feeling like shit warmed up, I'd spend a lot more time admiring his physique.

"Did we have sex last night?" I ask. Anthony smirks down at his bowl. "Bonetti. Answer me."

"Hmm do you think I jumped your bones before or after the car ride home, where you rapped WAP for me? *Twice.*"

"Nobody does a better Cardi B than me, *thank you.*"

Anthony chuckles. "I believe it. I saw it with my own eyes."

The tension screaming out of my skin isn't helping my hangover. Did we, or didn't we? I'm not sure what I want the answer to be. I mean, it's fine if we did, but what if I'd blacked out and not remembered what I was hoping would be amazing, animalistic sex with this piece of man meat? I don't feel sore except for my legs, which I assume is from my renditions of WAP. *Oh no.* Maybe his penis is so small that it left no reminder …

"Bonetti," I groan. "I'm spiralling."

Anthony chuckles. "We didn't have sex, Red. Chill."

A relieved sigh escapes my lips, and he raises an eyebrow. "That breath of relief is almost insulting."

"Your ego can take it," I dismiss. Anthony grins again and it makes me irrationally annoyed. "Why don't you look like you're dying?"

"I don't drink." Anthony scrapes his spoon around the bowl, the sounds resonating like nails on a chalkboard.

I grit my teeth as I press my nails into my scalp. "And you're here to rub it in?"

Anthony's smile widens as he places his now empty bowl in

the sink. He washes it and rinses it silently. I never realised how sexy it is watching a man clean up his own dishes until this moment. When he's finished, Anthony spins, his hands placed on the bench behind him. "How do you feel this morning?"

"Like shit."

"I know, but ... you're, alright?"

I narrow my eyes at him. "What does that mean?"

"How much do you remember of last night?"

My stomach drops. "That's never a good question to ask a woman with a hangover."

"Yeah, I don't think it's only a hangover," he says grimly. "One of the side effects of getting your drink spiked is memory loss."

I blink at him, something familiar yet vague dancing in my mind just out of reach. Like we've had this conversation before, but I can't remember it. "You think someone spiked my drink?"

"I think *Nathan* spiked your drink," Anthony snaps, his eyes flaring. "You could barely stand when I found you. That dick-head only had one thing on his mind, and it wasn't your wellbeing."

He gives me a run-down of what happened once we arrived at the studio and the sinking sensation in my stomach turns into something more violent.

"I want to throw up," I mutter.

Anthony surveys me. "I don't blame you. Whatever it was, knocked you around. I had to carry you inside once we got here."

My insides squeal with shame. "I'm so sorry."

The butterflies in my stomach batter their wings as Anthony's smouldering gaze lingers on mine. I forget that I'm hungover, too busy wondering what he's thinking when he looks at me like that.

"There's nothing to apologise for," he says finally, pushing off the bench. "Can't say the same for Nathan. He needs to watch his back."

"There's no proof he did anything."

"I might not have proof, but I don't trust the guy. Promise me you'll stay away from him." Anthony's face is etched with concern as he watches me.

"I promise to stay away from him if you promise to leave it alone," I reply. "No digging around by you *or* your brother. I want to keep my neighbours onside, especially since I haven't even opened yet."

Anthony sighs. "I promise."

"Thank you."

Anthony nods with apparent satisfaction before picking up his shirt, pulling it on over his head with ease. "I've gotta shoot off. You all good?"

Disappointment swells in my chest. "Yep. Thanks for ... everything."

He heads to the notepad and pen on the kitchen bench and spins it towards me. "While you were sleeping, I jotted down some websites and numbers for you."

I frown, walking over. "For what?"

"Recommended therapists. I had a number suggested to me when I moved here. Angela was just the first who could get me in."

I blink at him.

"In your garbling last night, you said you wanted to go back to therapy. You probably don't remember."

I rack my brain, remembering rambling about some narcissist bullshit. Vaguely.

"It was stuff about self-sabotage. You said you'd maybe consider going back—"

"Slow your roll there pal," I interject, squeezing the bridge of my nose. "I was on another planet last night. Sounds like I was talking out of my ass."

Anthony narrows his eyes, and I don't miss the slight shake of his head.

"What?"

He shrugs. "I've never met someone more in denial. And that's saying something."

My cheeks flame, unexpected embarrassment coursing through my limbs. "What's that supposed to mean?"

"There's nothing wrong with being scared of falling in love, Red. Most people are on some level."

Why is he bringing this up again?

"I'm not *scared* of falling in love," I argue. My hackles rise and any semblance of a schoolgirl crush dissolves before my eyes. "I like my freedom and the rush at the beginning of relationships more than *being* in one."

Anthony tips his head to the side, studying me. "Ah, yes. You've used that line on me before. The line we both know is bullshit."

My eyebrows spring to my hairline. "I don't have the energy for this today, Anthony. Get out of my house."

I turn away from him and march across the room, slamming my bedroom door closed, wincing at the bang it sets off in my brain, tears springing to my eyes.

I hate myself.

Anytime I'm hungover I hate myself, but this is the worst one I've had in a long time. I'm having to paint walls relentlessly with a headache that no number of painkillers seems to be able to fix. A hangover hits differently when the possibility of drink spiking is involved.

A part of me wants to report it to the police, but I'm still having a hard time believing Nathan did anything that sinister. Maybe the booze just went to my head, or the bartender made my drinks extra strong. Maybe I had more and just can't remember. Whatever happened, not being able to remember chunks of it is the most frustrating part. That and re-living the moments of me acting like a spoilt brat. And not only last night either, but the days and weeks leading up to today. I loathe how I've acted towards Anthony lately. He stopped last night from turning into something much more horrendous. He's been helping in the studio without me asking. He's looking out for me.

That I've used my own demons as an excuse for drinking too much and acting like an entitled obnoxious brat when I don't get my own way, is shameful.

Who needs therapy when you can analyse your own behaviour and tear yourself to shreds?

I've treated Anthony like crap, and I'll be lucky if he hasn't decided to void our bet and steer clear of me. I'd deserve it.

"Hey."

I stumble backwards from the wall, paint splattering down the front of my raggy old shirt.

Anthony Bonetti is standing silhouetted in the doorway.

19

ANTHONY

"HEY."

Kali stumbles backwards at the sound of my voice, a paint roller in her hand. I smile at the surprise on her face. She mustn't have heard me pull up.

I drink in the sight of her. There's no sign she's hungover. She's as stunning as ever. Her hair's piled on top of her head, locks falling out in random places. Her spandex shorts accentuate her muscular legs. Her old, baggy shirt is covered in flecks of paint, some of which have spilled onto her dark skin.

"How's it going?" I ask, eyeing the half-painted wall.

Kali follows my gaze and sighs. "You wouldn't know I've been painting for eight hours, would you?"

"Painting is slow, hard work," I reply. "You're getting there. *Patience*, remember?"

I swear Kali shudders as I utter the word.

"Patience. Yep, I'm practicing." She places the roller carefully into the tray. She dips into her pocket and fishes out the elastics I sent her in the mail, grinning at me sheepishly as she twirls them between her delicate fingers. "Look, I'm sorry—"

"Don't apologise. You don't have anything to apologise for."

She sighs. "Yeah, I do. I mean putting aside the shitshow that was last night, I'm sorry for my attitude the past few weeks. I've been way more highly-strung than I usually am."

I smile. "It's okay."

"It's not." She exhales deeply, like she has a lot to say. "I've got some issues, obviously. More than I realised. I'm sorry for acting like a brat. And for slamming the door in your face this morning."

"What did I just say? You don't need to apologise—"

"Accept the apology," she says through gritted teeth.

I smile and nod. "Apology accepted."

Kali gives me an awkward smile, before crouching down to pour more paint into the tray.

"Last night, you said that you went on the date because Nathan was nice to you. Which he wasn't, but that's beside the point." I crouch down level with her. "Do you really think I'm not nice to you? Because I never meant for anything I've said or done to be taken the wrong way."

"Well, there's no denying your mood swings are a struggle to keep up with," she replies, swiftly.

"*My* mood swings?"

"Yes!"

We both stand up at the same time, Kali waving the roller in her hand as she unleashes her anger. "One minute you're all *let's have a sex bet* and show up at my house and place of business whenever you feel like it. The next minute, you act like I insulted your mother and storm out of here. You refuse to answer my messages and phone calls, instead choosing to rock up here a *week* later and yell at me for being an idiot!"

I rub the back of my neck, the familiar sensation of discomfort crawling up it. "I'm sorry."

Kali's eyebrows spring to her hairline in surprise. "I was so not expecting that to come out of your mouth."

"I know when to apologise," I say with a shrug.

She glares at me. "Is that supposed to be a dig?"

"No, but I *am* sorry. I'm sorry for acting like a jerk. You ... triggered me." I bite my teeth together and a jolt of pain reverberates in my gums. It's a fruitless effort to control the pulse beating out of control in my jaw.

"I triggered you? How? What did I say?"

My hand rubs back and forth over my neck as nausea settles into my stomach. "Ah, shit."

"Look Anthony," Kali starts, her nostrils flaring. "I can deal with rejection or people losing interest. People have tastes and boundaries and can change their minds, but don't lead me on and then act like *this*."

I step towards her without hesitation. "None of that has anything to do with how I feel about you."

Kali's eyes widen before she clears her throat. "Well then, how did I trigger you?"

I sigh, tilting my head back to stare at the ceiling. My gaze trails across the lighting fixtures, stalling for time, searching for the right words—anything to save me from the inevitable story that must come out of my mouth.

"I'm an addict."

The words ring out loudly in the empty space. I don't take my gaze from the roof, instead I try to control my thunderous heartbeat, waiting to hear what Kali says next.

It's quiet. So *painstakingly* quiet, I wonder if she slipped out of the room without me realising.

"Okay."

I lower my head and see Kali watching me with interest.

"Okay?"

"Okay." She drops her roller into the tray before turning to me. "Keep talking."

I take a deep breath. "I've been clean for almost four years. Heroin, mostly." I hold my left arm out to her, covered in swirls of ink, as I had done with Hazel last year. Kali reaches out her hand and brushes it against my skin, a finger delicately running over the track marks I've done a solid job of covering. It's the first time someone other than myself or a nurse has touched them deliberately.

"I made life difficult for myself and the people around me for a long time," I admit. "I'm grateful I've still got my family and my health. For now, anyway. I never shared needles, thank Christ, and I've got a clean bill of health when it comes to STIs and blood-borne illnesses. Figure I should mention that with a sex bet hanging over us."

I don't mean it as a joke and she doesn't take it as one. Her gaze sears into my face as she processes the information. I'm acutely aware of the tension building in my shoulders, pulsating down to my clenched fists.

"I don't partake in most vices from my past anymore," I barrel on. "Drugs, alcohol. Occasionally, I'll smoke a cigarette, but that's as far as I've taken my bad habits. I go to therapy. I go to NA meetings when I need to. I have a sponsor I check in with. I'm sorry if that's disappointing or makes you uncomfortable. If you want to slow things down or back out of this, I'll understand."

My throat starts to dry as I wait for her to respond. She continues to blink slowly, a silent analysis occurring behind her eyes that I wish I could listen in on.

"I don't want to back out of anything," she finally replies.

A desperate breath of relief leaves my lungs.

"I'm surprised," she continues. "I had no idea. I'm a bit of a narcissist for not asking more about you. Or at least noticing that you don't drink until this morning."

"You didn't notice. I *told* you."

She glares at me and it's enough to break my face into a smile.

A look of realisation washes over her face and her hands come up to her mouth. "I'm an asshole. My comments the other day ... I can't believe I was so insensitive."

I shrug. "How could you have known?"

"In hindsight, it was a gross thing to say. I didn't mean to be so cavalier about something so serious. Those kids need help, and I wrote them off."

"I have no doubt they're shitheads, so don't feel guilty about that," I assure her. "But it's probably not *all* their fault."

We stand in silence, the weight of the words we've exchanged settling over us.

"I really am sorry," Kali repeats, closing her eyes. "About everything."

I curl my fingers around her wrist dangling at her side. "It's okay."

"I'm going to try and do better," she adds. "And I think the best way we can move forward together is if we *both* pick up a roller and start painting."

Her grin splits my mouth into another smile. I glance at my hand around her wrist and lift it up to sit between us, gently running my fingers across her palm.

"Sorry for acting like a moody dick," I mumble.

A chortle escapes Kali's throat. "Just like your brother."

"We might not share DNA, but we've got that in common," I agree.

I let my hand hold hers, not missing the way she gazes up at me from under her thick lashes. "Let's get to work."

20

KALI

Anthony and I work for the next few hours in comfortable silence. Music plays from the speaker and we both get lost in our own minds. I mull over what he told me about his past and I'm filled with gratitude. It mustn't have been easy for him to share his story with me, but I'm so glad he did. I feel humbled or trusted or ... something.

It's given me lots to think about, mostly about how I'd forgotten how good I've got it. How even though my parents may not have been my idols, at least I had Mimi and Baba for a short while. I grew up surrounded by love, guidance and discipline, and still managed to throw my privilege back in people's faces, especially those who've had it far worse than me.

Anthony and I work in tandem, both of us rolling white paint up and down the brick walls. Anthony moves the ladder around and paints the parts we can't reach from the ground. He hooks his legs around the rungs with such casual strength, it unnerves me. His shirtless torso flexes as he uses the roller, a light sheen of sweat coating him. To his credit, it doesn't appear he took his clothing off for my benefit (I also removed my baggy shirt an hour ago) because painting is hard work. However, it doesn't help my wayward imagination.

"Time check, Red?" Anthony calls from above me, tearing me from my daydreaming.

I glance at my watch. "It's nearly five."

"Shit. We've been at it for hours." I fight the urge to make some inappropriate remark at that comment as he deftly climbs down the ladder, balancing the roller in one hand. He reaches the bottom and places the head of it in the paint tray.

"My shoulders are killing me," he groans, rolling them back for release. The noise stirs something low in my belly as I watch his muscles contort.

"You've done too much for me already," I tell him. "Thank you. You should go and enjoy your Saturday night."

Anthony nods. "I plan on it. You wanna order in?"

"As in order food and … eat it together?" I clarify.

"Yep. That's what most people mean when they order in with other people."

"You were here all last night," I point out.

Anthony shrugs. "So? We've nearly finished this coat. Another couple of hours and we've done coat number twenty-three."

"I reckon we're up to coat thirty at least." I frown at the surrounding walls. The colour is *nearly* there, but it needs a couple more coats before I'll be happy with it.

"I guess with tattoos covering your body, most places on the Gold Coast won't let you in, right?" I tease, heading to retrieve my drink bottle. "That's why you spend your Saturday nights volunteering your time for women who desperately need it?"

"Yeah, it's either that or they look me up and see I have a criminal record."

I halt in my tracks and turn back to face him. "You still haven't told me why you went to prison."

"You still haven't asked."

Anthony watches me across the room, and I see apprehension in his eyes. There's a tightness to his face. Perhaps he's upset that he has to explain his history to new people. Maybe he's ashamed about whatever occurred in his past.

The need to assure him I don't think differently of him, no matter what happened, claws at my insides. I want to comfort him, let him know that we all have pasts to contend with. Unexpectedly, my vulnerability overwhelms me, and I talk.

"Did you know my dad had a heart attack?" I rush the words out, because I don't like hearing them and might back out of telling him everything. "He was a fit, healthy man. Loved to cycle and play sports. Never drank or smoked in his life. One day he just ... dropped to the ground and never got back up."

Anthony watches me, unmoving.

"I guess you could say my mum didn't cope too well once he died."

I shove my hands in my pockets, fingers grasping onto the elastics I now carry with me everywhere. I pull them out and stretch the fabric around the outside of my hands. I push them as tight as they will go, the fabric cutting into my flesh with satisfying pain. "Anti-depressants, alcohol, opiates. Whatever she could get her hands on. I was living with my grandparents about three months after my dad's funeral."

I clear my throat, my eyes stinging as I do my best to create the tree-like design I watched on YouTube earlier in the week. "Long story short, she ended up dying of liver failure about ten years ago. Plus side of both your parents dying, is they leave you a shitload of money."

A humourless laugh escapes my mouth. My fingers get stuck in the elastic knots. I attempt to pull my hands apart to unravel it, but it won't budge. I pull again, and again, and again, before a low grunt escapes my mouth.

And then Anthony is there, right in front of me. He cocoons my hands with his, stilling me. "Let me."

I can taste blood in my mouth from where I've bitten down on my lip and my eyes are watering. I fix my gaze on Anthony's hands, watching as he gingerly manoeuvres mine around the string, freeing them first, followed by the knot.

I don't care that a tear rolls down my cheek. I don't care that Anthony reaches his hand up and tenderly wipes it away. I force myself to look up at him and my body freezes, as if I'm caught in a trance-like state as the world around us becomes a blur.

"You can let people in, Kali," he whispers, curling my hands into his bare chest. He holds them there, his gaze never wavering from mine. "You can let *me* in."

I shake my head. "It's safer not to."

"Safer doesn't necessarily mean better."

Another tear splashes my lips with salt. Anthony gazes at me, his eyes ablaze with concern and something else I can't pinpoint.

"Your therapist has done a great job with you," I mutter. "You could be a life coach."

Anthony chuckles, squeezing my hands still cocooned at his chest. "I'm told I'm very good with my hands *and* my mouth."

I snort and try to pull my hands away, but he yanks at them with such force that our bodies collide with a resounding *slap*. Not a painful slap, but rather one that signals we're skin to skin, the sound echoing off the walls. There's no space between my stomach and the warmth of his exposed abs.

This is the closest I've been to him. His scent is magnificent. Like sweat and salt and *man*. His hooded eyes gaze down at me, his tongue dipping out to run across his bottom lip.

"We should order some food," I whisper.

"We really should."

Anthony holds my stare and adjusts his grip, keeping a grasp on both of my hands with one of his, while his right hand slides down the front of my sports bra to my exposed stomach. With a sudden jolt he shifts my body so that I'm straddling his right leg.

I gasp as the apex of my thighs grazes the hardened length tucked into the side of his pants. Anthony is silent, his eyes hyper-focused on my face.

Asking for permission.

My wordless, intense gaze gives him the answer he's searching for.

Anthony drops my hand so he can hold me steady at the waist. Both hands dig into my flesh as he pushes me down his thigh and pulls me back towards him, my most sensitive spot igniting at the friction against his length.

He steers me backward, and forward.

Backward.

Forward.

Every movement is white, hot heat shooting to my core. I reach my hands to his biceps to steady myself as he quickens the pace, moving my body like a rag doll over the bulge in his pants that's bursting to come out.

His mouth parts as he watches me, reminding me of when he pushed me against the wall outside. He wants to watch me as my pleasure builds, as my gasps become louder. He relishes watching me lose control. He gets off on the way my hands claw at his body, chasing the high, my body moving up and down his leg.

Any sense of logic or reason is swallowed by want and desperate need as I hungrily slide up and down him, the two of us falling into a rhythm that elicits pants from both our mouths. Anthony presses his forehead to mine, not breaking his gaze as he watches me. Neither of us dare make the move to kiss the other, but we continue this dance.

This dance of dry humping.

His large hands move to my ass as he keeps my rhythm in

check. He pushes his strong leg up into me; keeps it sturdy as I edge closer to my release.

Grinding over and over and *over*.

My gasps get louder as I get closer to my goal, a whimper escaping my mouth.

Anthony snaps to attention at the sound, something like a growl grumbling from his throat as he guides me. I grind myself against him unashamedly, too focused on the euphoric sensation I sense is *right there*.

Stars take over my vision and I cry out as my orgasm tears through me. I bite down onto Anthony's shoulder, and he hisses, clutching me close to him as I ride it out. He lets out a strained snarl, his body twitching underneath me.

When I come to, I lean back to see Anthony gazing at me, his eyes dazed.

"I reckon it's been about twenty years since someone made me come in my pants." He chuckles darkly and plants a chaste kiss on my forehead, before moving his leg away.

Instantly, I miss the contact, the warmth.

Instead of dwelling on that, I let out a deliberate breath to shake myself out of my stupor, the warmth of my high already fading. "Now I definitely need to eat."

Anthony laughs. "Let me change and we'll order something."

I smile as he heads out to his truck, a swirl of uncertainty coursing through me.

It was a harmless dry hump.

Nothing bad ever happened after a dry hump.

21

ANTHONY

WE DRY-HUMPED. Like teenagers. It was hot as fuck.

I didn't plan on that. On any of it. Once we started, I was just hoping to give Kali some release. However, as soon as she started grinding on me, I came embarrassingly quick.

The look in her eyes, the sounds she made when she moved against me. I've had a taste of it, and I want more. So much more.

On Fridays we get let off work at three, and I join my boss and a couple of the other guys on site for a drink at a local bar. I've never struggled with resisting alcohol since I got clean. I don't feel the urge for a beer that often and am happy being the guy who's clear-headed. Alcohol was never really my vice anyway.

"Alright, spill it, Peaches," Sonny, the site foreman demands as we slide into a booth.

"Spill what?"

"Don't *even* start that shit boy," he orders, rapping his knuckles on the table. "I *know* something happened with the firecracker. You've had pep in your step all day."

The work boys have got sporadic updates about Kali since I

started working with them. I can't help but talk about her with a shit-eating grin on my face most days. They give me a lot of crap for it and somewhere along the way they gave me the nickname Peaches because of it.

"Pep in my step?" I ask incredulously.

"You're acting all …" Sonny moves his arms to try to explain. "Loose and light."

"I just really love Fridays." I snicker as Sonny huffs out an impatient sigh. "Nothing's happened. Not really."

Sonny's eyes brighten. "Aha! So, something happened."

"What happened?"

Jared, another carpenter and Bill, my boss, join us with drinks.

"Nothing happened," I assure him.

Sonny scoffs, shaking his shaggy black hair out of his eyes. "Bullshit. Peaches got lucky."

Jared's mouth makes an 'o' shape as he plops down next to Sonny. "Finally!"

"I didn't get lucky."

"But *something* happened," Sonny insists. Jared leans in on his forearms, sliding a beer over to Sonny.

Bill sits down next to me with a tired groan and slides me a ginger beer. "Listen to you bloody gossips. Shut up and drink your beers."

"Cheers, boss," I say.

Sonny ignores him. "Come on. Details. You never give us details."

"I'm never giving you details."

Sonny grins. "She's working her vixen magic on you. You're going soft."

"God, you talk some shit."

Sonny feigns offence. "I am outraged."

"You are not." My phone buzzes in my pocket and I slide it out, unable to hide my elated surprise when I see Kali's name on the screen. "Sup, Red?"

"Bonetti, I need a favour." Her voice is a drug. She could ask me for anything right now and I'd do it.

"So soon? You've had a taste and now you want more?" Sonny leans in to listen and I shove my hand against his head.

"I knew it was a mistake to call you," she groans. "Forget it, I can't be—"

"Easy, easy. I'm only playing. What do you need?"

She lets out an exasperated sigh. "Is there any chance you can come to the studio? Like, right now? The electrician's meant to be here in fifteen minutes, but I got a call from the bank saying I missed a signature on a form. I've got to get back there before five o'clock, but preferably as soon as possible. Knowing my luck, it'll probably take ages to sort out."

I lean back to glance at the time, realising she's only got a couple of hours to get everything done. "Yeah, no problem."

"Thank you."

Kali pauses for an extra beat and my senses prickle. "What's wrong?"

"Those kids have been back," she murmurs.

A protective surge of anger charges through my body. "What happened? Are you okay?"

"I'm fine, but they spray painted the front; the roller door, the brick walls, the roof. They even waved to the camera when they finished." I hear the quiver in her voice that she's almost certainly doing her best to hide.

"I'll be there in a couple of minutes," I reply, taking another swig of my drink. "I'll take care of the electrician and you go do what you need to do. If you run into any strife, call me straight away."

"I will," she promises. "Thank you."

Bill has already stood to let me out as I hang up. Those bloody kids. They need a good scare to set them straight.

"Everything alright with the missus?" Sonny asks over his glass.

"Yeah, she needs my help with something," I reply, chucking cash on the table. "Thanks for the drink, boys."

"Nothing happened, but he's gotta run to her rescue," Jared mumbles to Sonny, loud enough for me to hear.

"Would you two shut up before I fire you?" Bill demands, gruffly. "Go help your woman, Peaches."

22

KALI

I HATE WINTER. It's a little after five p.m. and the sun has almost vanished behind the mountains. Short days. Bitterly cold nights. I'm sick of it already. I'm also sick of banks and forms and constantly worrying whether I can pull off having my own business.

And I'm sick of teenagers adding to that stress.

When I arrive back at my studio, the roller door is up and golden light streams out onto the entryway. I see Anthony inside, singing along to music as he paints the walls again. It should be one of the last coats we have to do.

We.

It takes me a minute to realise the hideous graffiti is gone and my heart swells. Not a mark is on the pristine brick frame. The eaves on the roof look freshly scrubbed. The ground looks like it's been hosed down with a water blaster.

An hour ago, I forced back tears of frustration and now, as I step instead, I force back tears of a different kind.

Anthony continues to push the roller up and down the wall. He's removed his shirt once again. Specks of paint are splashed on the side of his pants. It doesn't appear to bother him, or he hasn't noticed.

When he turns to add more paint to the roller, he notices me and reaches for the speaker to turn the music down. "Hey, how'd it go at the bank?"

"All sorted," I whisper, still gazing at him.

Anthony eyes me with caution. "Is everything alright?"

"You cleaned it all up." My voice is thick with emotion, but I'm too tired to try hiding it. Too overwhelmed by his generosity to put up a shield or pretend his acts of service don't mean more to me than I let on.

"Well, yeah. I didn't think it went with the aesthetic." He flashes a smile, before faltering. "I wanted to do it, so it didn't stain the paint job underneath. Don't start again about not needing help. It's not an issue."

I stare at him, this beautiful, kind man who makes my knees weak with one look. That admission increases my heart rate and my breaths become loud and deliberate.

Anthony watches me and places the paint roller on the ground. "Kali, I'm sorry. I didn't mean anything by—"

I don't think, I *move*, striding towards him with purpose. When I'm close enough, I fling my arms around his neck and crash my lips against his.

For a few seconds he stills, out of surprise, or shock, or confusion. I'm not sure. I'm just grateful he doesn't push me away as I drive my mouth into his so hard it hurts. When I step back from him, his mouth chases mine before he straightens up.

"You kissed me," he murmurs, his eyes fluttering.

"I did." Terror, dread, elation—every emotion known to man catapults through me. I dare not move in case I break whatever spell this is.

Anthony's gaze pierces mine. "I win."

I open my mouth to object, but it's swallowed by Anthony's

hungry mouth, devouring me, tasting me. He forces me back-wards, my legs nearly giving out as he rushes me and slams me into the solid brick wall. Cold, wet paint licks at my exposed shoulder blades as he crushes his rock-hard body against mine.

There's no space between us, but still, I want him closer. I grab at him, my nails digging into his flesh as I pull him into me. His tongue ravishes my mouth. The kisses are ferocious sending violent heat to my toes, making them curl.

Anthony pulls back to peer down at me, his eyes glazed as if he's drugged. He reaches a large hand up around my throat and gently squeezes, a small gasp escaping my mouth.

"You're going to pay for making me wait this long," he growls.

I grin up at him, grasping his wrist and guiding him to squeeze again. He obliges and my vision goes spotty for a few seconds. It's the perfect mix of discomfort and pleasure.

When he loosens his grip, my vision clears and he's staring down at me, his free hand sliding down my body to cup between my legs. I choke out a gasp, convinced he can feel how turned on I am through the fabric of my tights. His blue eyes are swirling with dangerous heat as his hand skims my waist-band and slips down the front of my tights.

As soon as his fingers rub against my skin, I groan. *Loudly.*

Anthony halts his hand in my pants, tensing at the sound. "Fuck, Kali. Don't make sounds like that."

"Or what?" I pant.

Anthony's hand moves from my throat to grip my jaw. It hurts in a good way. "Or I'll punish you."

My breath catches in my throat and Anthony grins as he releases my jaw and skates his lips across mine. I smile into his mouth, running my hands over his buzzcut and down the back of his neck.

I can't remember the last time I smiled into someone's mouth.

One minute, Anthony's slow and gentle, tasting every corner of my mouth with purpose. The next, he's gripping my face and head, as if he could climb inside my body if he tried hard enough. I peek at him so I can remember the look on his face as he breathes me in.

Anthony pulls me away from the wall and guides me to the floor, kicking supplies out of the way in the process. I laugh when the tray of paint flies out from under his foot and splashes across the old sheets acting as protection for the mats underneath.

"Shit." Anthony chuckles, looking at the mess at his feet. He chooses to ignore it and lowers himself to the ground, pulling me with him. Our bodies are now coated in splotches of white.

I'm still laughing as I straddle his waist. "You're buying me new paint."

"I'll buy you a whole fucking paint store," he growls.

Anthony pulls my face down to his, sweeping his tongue inside my mouth. A hum of pleasure echoes somewhere in the back of my throat as his hands comb through my hair and skim past my neck.

Our lips come apart so we can gasp for air and loose strands of my hair fall into his face. He brushes it away tenderly and looks up at me, running his thumb over my bottom lip.

The burning lust in his eyes halts my movements. For a moment I get lost in a spasm of panic and lean away from Anthony's mouth to take a quiet breath.

This is only sex.

I sit all the way up and peel off my top, unhooking my bra without further thought. As I slide it off, Anthony whimpers and drops his head to the floor. "Jesus."

I grin. "For future reference, that is always the correct response."

"You got it." Anthony sits up, his hands braced at my hips. He takes one of my breasts into his mouth and my head snaps back as he sucks. The contrast of his warm breath on my cool skin sends a tremor down my body. When he scrapes his teeth over my flesh, I hiss, digging my nails into his back and clawing down.

He bites down harder.

"Fuck you," I gasp, using both my hands to grab his face and tip it back to look at me. He's already grinning, his mouth wet with saliva and his eyes gleaming with promise.

With one hand still gripping his jaw, I reach down and deftly unbutton his pants, before stretching up on my knees to make more space. My hand tucks in behind the band of his briefs and Anthony sucks in a breath as it reaches in and skims his hardened length.

"Don't start something you can't finish," he warns.

"Who said anything about not finishing?"

I lift myself off him so I can rip his pants down his legs. Anthony helps from his lying position, kicking off his pants and his underwear. When I see him naked underneath me, my mouth goes dry. "Wow."

"For future reference, that is always the correct response." His smile nearly breaks his face. "And this seems incredibly unfair."

Anthony moves rapidly, coming out from underneath me. He curls a hand around my waist and shifts so he's behind me on all fours. He pauses for a beat and then he tears my tights down my legs, my underwear going with them. I swear I hear the fabric rip.

I think he's going to turn me to face him again, but instead, his movements slow. He runs his calloused hands down my back, as if he's tracing an invisible design along my spine to my tailbone.

"Your back is so sexy," he murmurs.

"My back?"

"Mmm hmm."

I'm acutely aware that I'm now completely butt-naked with my ass facing him, but he doesn't make me feel uncomfortable. He makes me feel wanted as he shifts to hover over me and kisses me softly on the shoulder.

I shudder.

He kisses me between my shoulder blades, a lick of his tongue hitting my flesh. He kisses a trail down my back, until he plants one on my ass. His hand massages a small circle on my right butt check.

He slaps me.

It's gentle and sends a shudder rippling up my spine. I *knew* he'd be the spanking type.

I peer over my shoulder at him. "Don't be gentle, Bonetti."

Anthony elicits a dirty chuckle. "You asked for it."

His words vibrate through my body.

Into my organs and limbs.

My hands splay out in front of me, and I suck in a giant gulp of air.

He rubs his hand over my butt cheek in a circular motion again, before lifting it and smacking me. It's a little harder but just as pleasurable. The tingle of the slap simmers on my skin, before he starts to rub it again. His hand disappears, until *thwack!* It's even harder than the one before.

His hand disappears from my skin, and I ache for the contact. When his hand collides with my flesh again, I let out a whimper and he rubs the skin to take the sting away.

"That's enough punishment for now," he whispers. "I'm not going to last much longer if I keep listening to those noises coming out of you."

He moves to roll me over, but instinctively I resist. "Take me like this."

He stills behind me, rubbing my lower back. "If that's what you want."

"It is." I keep my head forward, not brave enough to make eye contact with him.

Anthony nudges my knees further apart. I hear the tear of a wrapper and glance over to see him rolling a condom over his length. His toned, shiny torso covered in swirls of black that lead to his—

Oh, Lord.

I don't have enough time to appreciate the sight before me, because he nudges at my entrance. I turn back and inhale sharply, fisting the sheets beneath me. He teases me for a few strokes, before gripping my hips and leaning forward to whisper, "Brace yourself."

Anthony slams into me and I scream, not caring that anyone else who's decided to stay late might hear me. He grabs a fistful of my hair and wraps it around his hand, pulling my head up slightly. It's painfully good.

Anthony hammers into me relentlessly and I push up to meet him, inviting the pain and pleasure that ravishes my senses. He loosens his grip on my hair to grab onto my hips, digging into my flesh, and moving in and out of me with aggression, but it's not self-serving aggression. He's doing this for me. He's listening to every sound I make, tilting me at an angle that reaches so deep I nearly choke.

I grab at the sheets beneath, desperate for something to hold on to as the tingle in my belly starts to balloon.

"Yes, Kali," Anthony grunts. "Good girl. That's it." He slaps me on the ass again.

My orgasm tears through me out of nowhere. I see stars. I think I scream again. I'm not sure. I'm too busy revelling in the height of my orgasm and listening to Anthony grunting behind me, a snarl ripping from his throat as he reaches his climax.

I can hardly breathe as the two of us revel in the afterglow, Anthony's body curving over mine as he slows to a stop. He plants another kiss on my shoulder. "Victory never tasted so sweet."

23

KALI

I ROLL MY EYES, but I'm positively beaming. "You're going to be even more unbearable now, aren't you?"

Anthony pulls out of me, and I instantly feel empty at the loss. He manoeuvres me so we're both facing each other, lying on the paint-speckled sheets protecting the floor. "You'd better believe it, Red."

I curl my arms under my head and stare at him, basking in my post-orgasm bliss.

His eyes dart down as he skims my hip. "What does this mean?"

I know he's referring to my flower mandala tattoo. "The circle of life. Everyone has their own interpretations of mandalas, but that's what it represents to me. Life, creation, our place in the universe."

I got it the day I turned eighteen, much to Mimi's chagrin. Yoga and meditation were a big part of my life thanks to my therapist's recommendations. It was supposed to remind me to stay grounded when I felt lost.

I'd forgotten that.

Anthony's watching me and I blink away my thoughts,

giving him a smile. "You going to tell me what all your tattoos mean?"

"We'll be here all night. Not that I'd complain."

The intensity with which Anthony stares at me sends a sharp jolt to my chest. He reaches his arm out as if to pull me close to him.

I roll away. "I think maybe we should set some ground rules."

"Ground rules?" Anthony frowns. He watches me as I jump to my feet and slide my (thankfully intact) underwear back on.

"To make sure we're on the same page."

Anthony props himself up on his elbow. "I'm all ears, Red."

"Let's be practical about this," I suggest. "It's good right now because it's uncomplicated."

Anthony twists his lips. "And by instilling ground rules, you're *not* complicating it?"

I narrow my eyes. "Rule number one. No feelings. If we get feelings, we be honest and we end this."

Anthony studies me with a familiar look of suspicion, chewing on his bottom lip. "Why exactly do we have to end it if there are feelings?"

"Because I don't really do relationships," I reply, pulling my top over my head. I can deal with my bra later. "I get bored easily and I wouldn't want to make things awkward between us."

"Huh." His response is a sound of mild surprise, and he rolls his tongue over his teeth before nodding. "No feelings."

I ignore the pang of disappointment that fleetingly hums in my chest. "Good." I snatch up my drink bottle and take a swig. "We don't owe each other anything."

"So, we can see other people?"

I choke as the drink bottle slips from my hand, bouncing by my feet. I cough to clear my throat. "Sure. I've never been a big monogamy person. Use protection, shower before seeing me and we won't have an issue."

Anthony lets his head fall back and he runs a hand down his face. "Wow. Way to take the romance out of the situation."

"That's another thing. No romance. Romance leads to feelings. You're already forgetting the rules."

Anthony sits up, amused.

"What?" I snap. "You'll thank me later for initiating this conversation. Trust me. Don't you have any rules?"

He stares up at the ceiling in thought, twisting his lips as he muses. "I didn't realise I had to have a list ready."

Watching him lie there, sweat glistening on his chest as it rises and falls rhythmically, is almost hypnotising. A part of me wants to join him back on the floor and let him pull me into a vice-like embrace.

"Maybe I have one," he perks up.

"Have one what?"

"A rule." Anthony tilts his head to look at me, his blue eyes sparkling with mischief.

"Don't say it," I groan.

Anthony's mouth quivers. "How do you know what I'm going to say?"

"Because I know you. Because you're predictable and corny."

Anthony narrows his eyes in mock sincerity. "Don't fall in love with me, Red."

I sigh. "There it is."

Anthony unfolds himself from the floor, standing in one swift movement to tower over me. All muscles and tattoos and *nakedness*. "That's my only rule." His cobalt eyes search mine, maybe for a reaction to his words, patiently waiting for me to process what he's said. He leaves enough space between us to amplify the tension by a thousand.

It's taking every ounce of strength to ignore the press of his hardness against my hips. *His appetite is going to kill me.*

"I can agree to that," I whisper, holding his gaze. Anthony's eyes flash with something I don't recognise and my stomach lurches. It's as if hundreds and thousands of unspoken words linger and whirl around us, out of reach.

"Fine." Anthony breaks the spell by dropping his gaze to my lips. Silently, he drags his hand down the front of my torso, lifting the hem of my top. His fingers are hot pokers as they skim my exposed flesh.

Anthony watches his hand as it lowers into the front of my underwear. His gaze flickers back to mine as he runs his hand down to where I'm already wet. His eyes ignite with lust once again.

"Any more rules Miss Cooper, or are you done talking?"

I ignore the tiny voice in my head which whispers, *Girl, you are so fucked.*

24

ANTHONY

I'M FUCKED.

A couple of hours on the floor with Kali Cooper and she's all I can think about. When I wake up in the morning, I see her face. All day at work on the tools, I'm re-living the memories of our bodies entwined. When I head to her studio to help in the evenings, I hope she'll be there. I was thinking about her plenty before the amazing sex, but now that we've graduated to naked-ness and orgasms, my brain can apparently no longer think about anything else. *Healthy.*

I have no idea if Kali's thinking along the same lines as me. Lately I'll say something and prepare for a battle of wits, but instead of ripping into me, I'll see her processing thoughts behind her eyes. It's as if she's analysing situations and gets conflicted about sharing the outcomes she's arrived at.

Her unpredictability is something I love about her, but it's also the reason I've put off our date. Even though we made an agreement, she might decide to turn me down because of her rules. Or worse, she'll agree to go out with me out of pity and want to wrap the whole thing up as soon as possible.

"I don't think we've ever seen you this worked up." Sonny

scoffs into his plate of food across from me whilst Jared slurps a milkshake right in my ear.

"You haven't known me that long." I run my hand vigorously over my head.

It's Monday and we've been sent home early as it's raining, which is ideal for most people. You still get paid a full day's wages, but you can go do whatever you want. Lots of tradesmen head to the pub, or go home to watch Netflix, or brave the winds and hit the surf nearby.

Normally, I'd relish the chance to head home to work on my art pieces, or hit the gym to punch the bags, but not today. I'm so wound up I can't think straight.

Ever since that night with Kali, I've had pent up energy. We worked side by side in her studio all weekend, but her friends were there the entire time, and with her insistence on 'ground rules' plaguing my mind, I didn't dare make a move for fear it'd be interpreted as crossing the line.

Sonny and Jared dragged me to a local diner for lunch, sensing I was on edge, but I'm not sure it's helping. My leg won't stop bouncing. I need to go to a meeting after this and maybe even a run to clear my head.

"You wanna talk about it?" Jared asks, nudging me in the ribs. "I know we're gossips, but we can be helpful. Sometimes."

I chew on my lip and quickly decide I don't care what sort of backlash and teasing I get for spilling my guts. "Kali and I slept together."

It takes a full minute for Sonny and Jared to stop cheering, roaring and banging on the table like animals. When Sonny finally sinks back into his chair, his smile nearly breaks his face. "You should be stoked, Peaches. Why do you look like a sad sack?"

"I'm not a sad sack," I argue. "She implemented rules, and it rattled me."

Jared frowns. "What do you mean?"

"She established rules. Laid out very clear boundaries. She's protecting herself."

"That's good, right?" Jared asks. "She's being clear about where she stands, so you can both be on the same page."

Sonny shakes his head. "Wait, wait, wait, what sort of rules?"

"No feelings. No romance. We can see other people."

Jared lets out a low whistle. "Sounds like Sonny's dream girl."

Sonny barks out a laugh. "You're not keen on the rules, Peaches?"

My swallow crackles in my ears. "I respect her rules, but it's totally thrown me off my game. I've got no idea what I should or shouldn't be doing."

That's partially true. I don't know where I stand with this woman. She's taking up so much space in my brain it's hard to function, but it's not just that. I wanted to reach out and touch Kali all weekend. I wanted to steal her away and be alone with her. I wanted to make sure no other man even *thought* about looking at her the way I do. The very thought of Nathan still working in her vicinity made my blood boil. I've still got half a mind to pay him a visit one of these days.

"Sounds like you need to play her at her own game," Sonny muses. "Don't give her the feelings or romance. See other chicks. She'll get jealous eventually."

"I'm not into mind games," I grumble.

And I don't want to see other chicks.

"Don't listen to him," Jared says. "He's an idiot."

Sonny nods his agreement.

"Be yourself, man," Jared continues. "There's no way she'll be able to resist you with your tattoos and your broken, mysterious vibe."

"Shut up." I throw a napkin at him, and he laughs.

"Mate, I might not have known you for that long, but I'm

pretty sure you could score any woman you wanted. Kali is no
exception. She just might make you work harder for it."

"I do love a challenge."

"She's gonna break you," Sonny says matter-of-factly.

My phone buzzes on the table, interrupting my chance of a
flippant response.

Speak of the devil.

RED

> Word has it that you won a bet and are too
> chicken shit to ask me out now.

ME

> I knew you wanted me

RED

> Gag.

ME

> And I knew you were into gags

RED

> You are so predictable

ME

> We'll see. Saturday, 12pm. Wear comfortable
> shoes.

RED

> Oh, Jesus. What activity are you taking me on?

ME

> Do what I say, or I'll bring a gag to our date.

RED

> You say that like it's a bad thing.

My stomach somersaults and I grin at my screen. Sonny scoffs
in the background. "She's *definitely* going to break you."

25

ANTHONY

IT's days like today I'm grateful I shaved my head.

The amount of excess energy coursing through my body has produced never-ending sweat all morning. Even an hour at the gym boxing out my angst, only did so much. I caught myself pacing as I waited for Kali to confirm our date and spent way too long deciding whether to wear a black or grey shirt. Imagine having to style hair on top of that.

Even now, as I stand on Kali's doorstep waiting for her to answer the door, my hands are sticky. I can't remember the last time I felt this scattered.

Maybe when you were off your face on drugs, a voice mutters in my brain. I scoff to myself. At least I can shrug off those voices these days.

The front door swings open and Kali comes into view, her presence knocking the wind out of me. "Wow."

Kali is sexy in anything but seeing her in jeans and a tight-fitting top that exposes a slither of flesh is tantalising. Her dark hair spills over her shoulders, tumbling onto her breasts. She bites her lip in apparent shyness as I assess her.

"Thanks. You look ... good." Her gaze travels down the long-sleeved grey shirt I decided on, hovering at the tattoos peeking out at my wrists. Her cheeks flush in the afternoon sun and I desperately want to know what dirty thought entered her brain.

"You're doing wonders for my ego." I lean in and kiss her on the cheek. I love the way her breathing hitches. "Shall we?"

I lead Kali by the hand along her garden path towards the road.

"Tell me you're not doing the stereotypical bad boy thing and riding a motorcycle?" Kali asks, eyeing the motorbike parked ahead of us.

"Of course not," I reply. "Motorcycles are impractical and expensive."

"And Patrick won't let you have one?"

I give a friendly slap on her perfect ass. She jumps and tries to swallow a squeal of delight, but I hear it before she can stifle it.

"Unfortunately, we're in my boring old truck today."

Kali smiles. "I like your boring old truck."

I unlock it and head to the passenger side to open the door for her. When she brushes past me, I inhale her scent. "Ma'am."

She peers at me. "I don't know how to take this gentlemanly side of you."

"I'm always a gentleman." I lean in and my nose skates the shell of her ear. "*Most* of the time." I nip the edge of her ear and don't miss her quiet gasp.

"Where are we going?" she whispers.

I lean back and smile at her. "To my favourite place."

26

KALI

"CAN we stop and appreciate that your favourite place is watching people run and jump off a cliff?"

Anthony leans back on the picnic blanket with a dazzling smile, his eyes hidden behind his dark sunglasses. "It's not like they're plunging to their deaths."

"But they *could*."

Anthony drove for almost an hour, the two of us spending most of the car journey talking about his job and my studio and bickering about each other's music choices. When we weren't doing that, I was busy trying to control my breathing anytime Anthony looked at me. Which was a lot.

We eventually arrived at a western-facing clearing at the top of Tamborine Mountain, where several small groups of people were sitting having picnics or taking photos of the view. The most exciting part, however, was the handful of people running and jumping off into the wind, gliding around off the cliff face and defying all laws of logic.

Anthony retrieved a picnic blanket and a basket packed with goodies from his backseat, and set us up wordlessly on the grass, facing out to the cliff drop. I'd be lying if I didn't swoon at the thoughtfulness of it.

"Why haven't you jumped yet?" I ask, stuffing a grape into my mouth. "Too busy being a little pussy ass bitch?"

Anthony barks out a laugh and I grin at him, peeking down to see if he's still squeezing a stress ball in his hand.

He is.

He's been doing that since we sat down, and it makes me wonder if he's nervous.

"Every time I visited from Sydney, I'd come up here and watch them for hours. Never felt the urge to sign-up for it. I enjoy the peace of watching."

I get what he means. They're almost hypnotic, the way they run and leap with grace, directing their gliders through invisible waves. It's soothing to the soul, watching the way they dip up and down, the smiles on their faces evident each time they come back in.

"Don't know if hang gliding would suit your bad boy persona," I muse. "I mean, it's pretty ballsy, but most of these guys are wearing spandex. Not sure that's your style."

Anthony removes his sunglasses and I sigh at the sight of his blue eyes, squinting at me with curiosity. "What's my style?"

"Black, white, grey. Tattoos. You'll take any excuse to get your shirt off."

Anthony chortles. "Anything else?"

I shrug. "You know. Bad boy stuff. Smoking on occasion, boxing, fights, pr—"

I catch myself before I say the next word, but the quirk of Anthony's eyebrow signals he knows what I was going to say.

"Prison?" he offers.

"I didn't mean—"

Anthony chuckles and sits up, stealing a grape out of my hand. "What do you want to know, Red?"

"What did you do to end up in prison?"

Anthony sits up straighter, gazing out at the horizon. "I got done for drug possession."

"How old were you?"

"Twenty-five. Looking back, I'm surprised I wasn't in there sooner, or for longer."

"What's it like?"

Anthony stares straight ahead. "I had it pretty easy. I was at the bottom end of C Class and went to a farm jail, meaning I got to work. If I had to sit around playing cards and making chitchat, I would've died of boredom."

"Is that where you learned your trade?"

"Yep. Had a great mentor in there too. Kept me out of trouble while I was inside."

I'm relieved he didn't come out with a horrific prison story you often hear about from documentaries and horror movies. "Does prison work?"

Anthony scoffs. "Well, I never went back after my stint and that was ten years ago."

"That's good."

"Prison didn't change me. I just got better at not getting caught." He shakes his head as if he's thinking back to his younger self. "I only spent nine months in there. That's nothing compared to what it could've been. I think Patty hoped I'd straighten myself out, but instead, I became a headache for him. For almost ten years, he's stressed about me. I think he's stressed about me since the day we met."

I don't miss the guilt riddled on Anthony's face, the way his lean arms flex with tension.

"So, what straightened you out?"

"Patty's incessant, overprotective nature. Therapy." Anthony takes a deliberate breath, before exhaling loudly. "Chloe."

My ears prickle at the mention of that name. Hazel mentioned a Chloe during last year's fallout with Patrick. From memory, she was his ex-girlfriend and died in a tragic accident, but she didn't mention her again.

Anthony turns his body towards mine. "Chloe was Patrick's girlfriend. She and I were on the couch together one day when Patty was at work. A car came flying through the living room window and took her out before I knew what happened. God knows how it missed me."

He looks like he wants to say more, but the internal struggle is so evident on his face, that I place a hand over his. "It's not your fault, Anthony. Shit happens sometimes."

Anthony's eyes dart to mine, pain riddling his features. The pulse tics so vehemently in his jaw, I'm almost certain he could burst apart at any minute.

"We don't have to keep talking about this," I assure him. "But I'm glad you told me."

Anthony's eyes glisten. "Me too."

My gaze darts to the ball which he's squeezing vehemently in his fist. I touch his hand and he uncurls it, allowing me to take the ball. "I haven't got a stress ball in my collection yet."

Anthony finally smiles and my chest almost bursts with the relief on his face. "Is your collection helping?"

I reach into my jeans pocket and pull out the elastics he sent me. "They're never far away from me these days. A distraction I never knew I needed." I glance at him. "Is that why you sent them to me? Because you knew I needed a distraction?"

Anthony's gaze slams into mine. "I sent you those things so you wouldn't forget about me."

My heart skips a beat.

Without thinking twice, I lean in and kiss him firmly on the lips, the butterflies in my ribcage battering furiously. His hand skims my jaw and finds its way into the hair at the nape of my neck, shooting a dance of tingles down my spine. He guides my mouth open with his tongue, sliding it across my bottom lip and pulls me closer to him. My leg accidentally knocks over the glass bottle of apple juice in the process.

"We knocked the apple juice over," I murmur against his mouth.

He pushes my hair back off my face. "Fuck the apple juice."

27

ANTHONY

"I LOVE TO WIN." Kali bats her eyelashes with a smirk on her face.

"I can tell."

She smiles smugly, holding a fluffy red lobster toy under her arm.

After our picnic and make out session on Tamborine Mountain, I managed to pull myself away from Kali and pack us into the truck. We drove back to the Coast, my hand on her thigh for most of the journey. She traced the tattoos on my wrist and fingers absentmindedly and fuck if it didn't feel awesome. I could've driven like that for hours.

I ended up pulling into an arcade a few suburbs away from Kali's house, thinking a bit of competition couldn't hurt on our first date. We made everything into a game, especially the basketball and racing challenges.

She wiped the floor with me. But I didn't care.

I've felt a small sense of relief since we spoke earlier. Relief that I've spoken to her about Chloe but guilt I didn't tell her all of it. I didn't tell her Chloe and I were high at the time or that the suggestion to get high was my idea. I don't know if she'll want to see me again after telling her the truth.

"Ooh, a photo booth!" Kali cries, clapping her hands. "Let's take some to remember the night I absolutely *destroyed* you in an arcade."

I roll my eyes, letting her pull me towards the tiny booth. She clambers in and I follow suit, squeezing into the tiny space and closing the curtain to seal us in. "I haven't been in one of these in twenty years."

Kali punches away at the buttons. She's so light and carefree tonight, like she needed a night away from the constant slog of renovations.

"Ready?" she asks. "You're allowed to smile."

The screen starts to countdown from three and Kali's already in prime position, her tongue poking out and the lobster teddy she won at my expense clutched to her chest. I can't tear my eyes away from her.

When the photos shoot out, she whips them out before frowning at them. "You're looking at me in all these," she mutters, running a painted nail over the strip. "Try again. Give me something, Bonetti. Apart from intense brooding."

Kali presses at the screen for another round of photos, settling back with a smile. After the second flash I scoop my hand around her neck, pulling her towards me. Her big eyes widen for a split second, before she's grabbing my face with both hands, pulling me down over her. Her lobster toy falls to the floor, forgotten.

A moan hums from her throat into my mouth and my hand flexes, gripping her hip. "We're in public," I remind her. "You can't make noises like that."

Her eyes flutter open, her lips red and swollen from where I've mauled her. "You started it." She grabs the front of my shirt and pulls me back to her, her tongue greedy as she slips it into my mouth.

I readjust us so she's straddling my lap, my hands curving underneath and planting on her tight ass, squeezing her *hard* so she gasps, her lips breaking away.

"I've wanted to do that all night." I reach up and run kisses down her neck.

Kali leans back to allow me space. "Why didn't you?"

"Because I'm a gentleman."

Kali rolls her hips into my lap. I grunt and still her hips. "You're going to make me come from dry humping *again*. In public, this time."

She grins at me before slowly, rolling her hips again. I hiss and grab the front of her jeans, startling her. I unbutton her pants with one hand and slide my hand inside, fingers tracing over satin. Our eyes never leave the other's, our breaths coming in erratic hot puffs. Her fingers grip the back of my head in anticipation, and I take that as my cue, pushing her panties to the side and dipping my fingers lower.

She whimpers as I run my fingers over her, and I bite her bottom lip. "You're soaking."

"Quit bragging," she pants, her body pushing into my hand. I let the palm of my hand rub back and forth and she tips her head back. "Fuck."

I slip one finger inside and she gasps, stilling as she hunches over my shoulder. Her teeth sink into my flesh through the fabric.

"You all good?" I whisper into her ear, pushing her hair aside.

Kali holds my head in a vice-like grip, her breath quivering. "More."

My breath hitches, but I obey her like a man drugged. I slide another finger inside her and she clenches around me. The fact that anyone could open the curtain, that my shoes sticking out makes it obvious what we're doing, doesn't bother either of us. It only heightens the situation.

"You're greedy," I murmur, slowly moving my fingers in and out of her.

"I'm a woman who knows what she wants." Kali's breathless gasps fill the small space and my dick strains against my pants. It's taking every ounce of self-control I've mastered over the past few years not to strip off and do the deed right here.

We fall into a rhythm, Kali moving with me as I swirl my hand in and out of her, fast, then slow, then fast again. When she picks up the pace and her moans become less controlled, I can tell she's close.

"Shhh," I whisper, chuckling under my breath. "We're going to get sprung if you don't keep it down."

"I don't give a fuck," she breathes, kissing me again. Her hands are everywhere, grasping and pulling at my clothes as she climbs to her climax. When she reaches it, her fingernails claw into my skin, scratching down my arms as she bites my neck. A hiss escapes my lips at the pleasurable pain, my hand slowing its pace until we're both heaving, my fingers still inside her.

Kali sits up and looks at me, eyes glassy, lips red raw. I slowly remove my fingers from her, sliding my hand out of her panties. Before I can overthink it, I open my mouth and take my fingers all the way in, watching her as I run my fingers over my tongue.

Kali's mouth parts, stunned. She watches me with an intensity that pierces through my skin. I make a resounding pop as I remove my fingers from my mouth and lick my lips. "Delicious."

Kali shakes her head and repositions herself to sit next to me again. Rosy-cheeked and breathless, she reaches for a couple of coins in her purse and slots them into the machine.

"You all good?" I ask again.

"Yep." The countdown on the screen starts. "I want a permanent keepsake to remember this moment." She snuggles into the crook of my arm and smiles at the camera.

I'm too busy grinning down at her when the first flash goes off.

28

ANTHONY

KALI'S STUDIO LOOKS MINT.

The walls are finished now that I've repainted where we smeared them. The floor protection has been lifted and rubber mats are fitted to the back part of the studio where the equipment will go. The front desk is finished, complete with white panelling and a timber benchtop. Once the signage is up, the place filled with reformers and mirrors, and Kali's finishing touches, it'll be almost ready to go. There's just one thing that's getting in the way of Kali's success and I'm about to deal with it the only way I know how.

I make sure to lock the place up and park my car out of sight while I wait. Those little shits are predictable. They've been hitting Kali's studio on the same days at the same times. Young Anthony would've taught these kids some valuable lessons in how to change up routine and minimise getting caught.

Sure enough, after twenty minutes of sitting in my car, the three of them round the corner on their pushbikes. Hoods up, a bag slung over one of their shoulders. They look around before dropping their bikes and getting out their equipment. Spray cans. Original.

They spread out and start painting something on the roller door and I jump out of my truck, creeping up until I'm just behind them, listening to their snickering.

"If you guys are gonna graffiti this place, at least do it with something original. Your tag sucks."

The three of them spin at the same time and I snap a photo, before tossing my phone on the ground. As one of them lunges for me, I pull the pin on the fire extinguisher under my arm and spray the three of them with vigour, satisfaction filling me as they start to screech and cough.

It was a light spray, really. Enough to give them a fright. "Don't move."

Their eyes blink through the white coatings on their faces and it takes all my will not to keel over laughing at the sight of them. It wouldn't be hard for them to flee. I'd only be able to zero in on one of them anyway, but this was the best I could do, that was on the tamer side of the illegal scale anyway.

"You guys are going to clean this up, right now."

"Eat me," one of the boy's spits.

I smile at him without humour, and it has its desired effect. His glare falters. "Do as I say, or we're going to have a very big problem, *Jason*."

Jason flinches this time and looks between his two mates. "H-how-"

"Do I know that you live on New Cavender Street with your mum and younger sister, Lucy?" I ask. "That you became friends with Sean and Tyler here in grade seven and the three of you have been acting like dickheads ever since? Great questions."

I have them right where I want them. Having Patty's connections and resources to investigate people is an advantage I've taken for granted. Getting to help with one of his cases last year and now living together full-time, it wasn't exactly rocket science before I tracked down a history of each of these teenagers.

Lots of this isn't legal, but I'm hoping they're too scared to do anything about that.

I nod my head to the cleaning supplies I left out next to the post, the fire extinguisher still pointed. "Get scrubbing'."

They hesitate. Sean and Tyler look to Jason for what to do next. Reluctantly, Jason reaches for the cleaning supplies and the three of them begin washing off their handiwork. They're silent apart from their loud sighs and huffs of frustration.

After ten minutes, they're tired. "This is bullshit," Jason moans.

"You know, if you pulled this shit in prison, you'd take one hell of a beatdown," I said. "Be grateful this is all I'm threatening you with."

"You've been to prison?" Jason asks. For the first time this evening, I see his hard exterior crack.

"Yes."

"Shit," Sean mutters. "What's it like?"

Based on accounts from a lot of people, my experience wasn't the worst. I was a first-time offender in a low-security prison. I had plenty of leisure time outside, was allowed access to the gym, library and classes, and the food was tolerable. I had a couple of run-ins with some of the other inmates, but my early years in the foster system and protecting Patrick at school had already taught me how to hold my own.

But it wasn't a walk in the park. Being told what to do every minute of the day. When you could sleep, when you could piss, when you could make a phone call to a family member. Knowing you had zero control and freedom inside that space. That one foot wrong could extend your sentence for any given amount of time.

"I wouldn't recommend it," I reply. "But the way you boys are going, you've got a one-way ticket to the best ones in the country. Keep it up, you'll be there by the time you turn eigh-teen. The boys in there would love fresh meat like you."

Sean's eyes bulge out of his head as he turns back to scrub-bing. Jason and Tyler glance at each other warily.

"What did you do to end up in prison?" Tyler asks. "You kill someone?"

Pictures of Chloe flash through my mind. I might not have gone to prison after that fateful day, but my chaotic and disrup-tive behaviour before that led to it all happening.

"I did a lot of drugs for a long time," I admit. "And someone I cared about died because I was a fucking mess. Prison was a walk in the park compared to that. Trust me. You don't want to go down that road."

The three young men are silent. I notice Sean assessing me, his gaze dragging over my tattoos properly for the first time. I had hoped that if I showed up with my ink exposed, it might be a bit more threatening for at least one of them. Sean already looks like he's second-guessing his life choices.

"I get that this was your place to hang out, but you boys have got to get over it," I continue, lowering the extinguisher. "Find somewhere else to get drunk or high. Better yet, stop getting drunk and high. I know it's fun, but it's a slippery slope to hell."

The three of them exchange glances again and I take the lull as an opportunity to push my point home.

"There's a drop-in centre a couple of blocks from here," I tell them. "If you can't go home or you're struggling, there's some people there who can help."

"Calm down, Pops," Jason snaps. "We smoke a bit of weed now and then, but we're not junkies." He glances at his friends before sighing begrudgingly. "We were paid to do this."

I straighten up, narrowing my eyes. "What do you mean you were *paid*?"

"He said not to tell," Tyler hisses.

Jason shrugs, pointing at me. "This guy has been to jail. He can deal with him."

"Take care of *who*?" I demand, but I already know the answer before it comes out of his mouth.

"Old mate from the pool shop," Jason replies, pointing his thumb over his shoulder. "Nathan. He came up to us one night. Said he heard about how we wrote her a note and wanted us to do some other shit to scare the chick that owns this place. We weren't really interested at first. The note was something we did on a dare, but he said he'd give us each fifty bucks every time we did something to set her back."

A small grin breaks out on Jason's face, and I can't help it as I reach out and slap him up the back of the head, my blood pulsating in my ears.

"Ow!"

"You're lucky that's all I'm doing to you," I hiss, before nodding to the cleaning products. "You ain't leaving until every scrap of paint is off that door and if you destroy anything else of Kali's or come anywhere *near* her again, remember I know where each of you live. And if you know what's good for you, you'll stay away from Nathan too. You don't want to be on the wrong side of this when I'm through with him."

For the first time tonight, I see their youth shine through their eyes. They each look scared and worried in their own way, and I have no doubt that the venom and hatred in my eyes and the tone of my voice has made each of them realise this has gone beyond a few silly pranks.

"Get back to work." Silently, they obey, and I stand there until they've scrubbed every speck of paint off, stewing over the fact Nathan has been paying these kids to destroy Kali's property, presumably because he's pissed off at how their date ended.

When I'm satisfied that everything is clean, I let them collect their bikes. As they cross the parking lot, Sean turns back. "We never meant to really scare her, you know."

I don't respond out of fear I'll explode in a fit of rage and wait until they're completely out of earshot before I let out a giant exhale, my hands trembling with rage.

I force myself to head back to my car, my gaze repeatedly shifting to the shopfront at the end of the lot.

As I climb inside the cab, I reach for my phone and dial immediately.

"Hello?"

"Patty. I need a favour."

29

ANTHONY

"You sure you want to do this?"

My gaze follows my brother's out the window towards the suburban house at the end of the dark, quiet street. We're in one of Patrick's cars, this one a Tesla he only uses in these sorts of situations. It works because its engine is quiet and it won't stand out on the Gold Coast, especially in this neighbourhood.

"He drugged her and paid some kids to mess around with her. I'm sure."

Patrick nods, still looking out the window, no doubt surveying for witnesses and any potential risks. "Stick to the plan. We get in, we do it, we get out. We don't tell Hazel or Kali about this, understood? It puts them at risk if they know anything."

And they'd kill us both.

"Understood."

That's good enough for my brother. He nods, signalling it's time to go, and we quietly climb out of the car.

My heart thunders against my ribcage as we approach the house with the stealth of panthers, slipping into our old patterns with such ease it's almost alarming.

Patrick and I flirted with the edges of the law during our time working undercover. It was such a necessary part of the job that even Patrick's captain turned a blind eye on most occasions. If we had to rough up a couple of bad guys, it was an unspoken rule to proceed, but with caution. AKA don't get carried away and don't be stupid enough to get caught.

Patrick's been so hellbent on being "a good person" lately, I was surprised he agreed mere minutes after I explained the situation over the phone, but he had my back immediately. We hatched a simple, yet effective plan and an hour later, here we are.

Steam puffs out of my mouth in front of me as we reach the side door as planned. Patrick keeps a vigilant eye and ear out as I step forward, retrieving my tools from my backpack. In about ten seconds, I've picked the lock and gently slide the door open.

We step inside and close the door behind us and head straight to where we know the master bedroom is, thanks to the quick Google of the floor plan prior to arrival. I can hear that dickhead's obnoxious snores from down the hallway.

We enter his room, and he doesn't flinch, which is a good thing. It's going to make this much easier. I glance at Patrick who nods, and I round the bed to shake Nathan awake.

I give him a violent jolt and his snoring halts abruptly. He blinks up in confusion at my face and I smile at him. "Hello, sleeping beauty," I murmur. His eyes widen and a fraction of a scream escapes his mouth before I punch him in the face, and he's knocked out cold.

"Ow," I grumble, shaking my hand.

Patrick chortles under his breath. "Let's move him before he wakes up again."

Nathan groans as his eyes flicker open. It takes him a couple of seconds to register what's happening; to gather his senses from his chair in the middle of his dining room. He wriggles against the restraints and breathes heavily through his nose as he focuses on me, then Patrick standing in the corner of the room.

He makes a long, whiney noise from behind the duct tape, and I slap him across the cheek, silencing him instantly. "Don't do that. You'll just drag this out longer than it needs to be."

Nathan continues to breathe erratically, and I pull a dining room chair to sit across from him. The fear in his eyes is so much more satisfying than I imagined it to be.

"Let's not fuck around," I explain to him. "We're going to ask you some questions and we want your honest answers, Nathan. The more honest you are, the less painful this will be for you. Do you understand?"

Nathan continues to hyperventilate, glancing over at Patrick before looking back at me.

"Do you understand?" I repeat.

He nods frantically.

"Good." I reach to the dining table and pick up a pocketknife. Nathan throws his head back, as if leaning back from me will somehow help. "Now, I'm going to remove the tape from your mouth. If you scream or shout for help, I'm going to take this knife and stab it through your hand. Are we clear?"

Nathan's eyes are now wide with panic, but he nods in agreement.

I whip the tape off, almost willing him to scream out, but he remains silent except for his heavy breathing. Then I scoop up the vial of tablets Patrick found in the bathroom while I was tying him up.

"Do you sleep well, Nathan?" I ask, twirling the bottle between my fingers.

He narrows his eyes, confused. "What?"

"Did I stutter?"

Nathan's eyes widen in panic again. "Yes. Yes, I sleep well."

I nod. "These helping?"

Nathan's gaze lands on the bottle in my hands and the remaining colour drains from his face. "My doctor prescribes me those."

"I can see that. Your kind doctor prescribes you gamma-hydroxybutyric acid. For what, exactly?"

He swallows. "I have narcolepsy."

I flash my teeth in an almost maniacal way at him, waving my knife in the other hand. "Come on, Nathan. Remember what I said about being honest?"

He grimaces as I lean towards him, watching beads of sweat roll off his head. "You don't use this for narcolepsy, do you?"

"No."

"You use this to drug women, don't you?"

He grits his jaw. "Yes."

"You used this on, Kali." I hold the bottle up, the mere sound of Kali's name coming out of my mouth reinvigorating my earlier rage. "You drugged Kali with GHB, didn't you?"

"*Yes,*" he hisses.

His admission reassures me that breaking into his home wasn't a mistake. That we haven't taken a risk for nothing. That this piece of shit deserves way more than the fright Patrick and I are giving him.

Patrick clears his throat from behind me and it takes every ounce of willpower to lean back in my chair, and not crash tackle this weasel to the ground.

Patrick comes into my peripheral vision, his phone in his hands. "I've been doing some digging on you Nathan. Fraudulent payments, outstanding debts. You haven't filed a legitimate tax return in four years."

"Tax evasion. That's what they got Al Capone on." I wink at Nathan.

Nathan looks murderous but keeps quiet as Patrick continues. "Putting aside your questionable business ethics, you seem like a genuine piece of shit. Amelia Falconio, Taylor Brown, Chelsea Thorne, Erin McCullough, Ari Adams. Any of these names ringing a bell?"

Nathan's mouth quirks at the edge. "Maybe."

"These women were hospitalised," Patrick forges on, level-headed. "Injuries from suspected sexual assault they couldn't remember, because they all had GHB in their systems. All after having some sort of interaction with you."

"There's no proof I did anything to those women," Nathan rasps, tilting his chin up at Patrick. I flick the pocketknife in my hand and Nathan glances at it. "But now that you mention it, yeah, I might've helped them along a little."

"You're a scumbag," I spit.

Nathan glares at me before sighing. "What do you want?"

That's the million-dollar question. What I *want* is to beat this guy into oblivion and drop him over the edge of a cliff so no one will have to worry about him again. Much as that thought might bring me temporary satisfaction, it's not who I am.

Realistically, we didn't need to come here tonight. Patrick could've tipped off his old police colleagues about his criminal activity and left it at that. But it wasn't enough. Not for me. That might make me selfish, but I wanted to hear the truth with my own ears, see him squirm under my own hand.

"You need to leave town," I reply. "Immediately. Pack up your shit, get rid of your business and never come back. You're never to lay a finger on Kali or any other woman without their complete, sober consent."

Nathan grunts, leaning back as if he's thinking about his options. "And if I don't?"

I smile, flicking the blade between my fingers. "I guess you could stick around and find out."

Nathan's chest rises sharply. "I'll leave."

Patrick nods at that and tilts his head at me, signalling to wrap this up before we test our luck and overstay our welcome.

Begrudgingly, I undo Nathan's restraints and step away with disgust, tossing the items into my bag. "One word of this to anyone and it'll be the last thing you do."

Nathan grunts again, a smirk plaguing his arrogant face. "Whatever."

My fingers twitch at the urge to throw another punch in his face, but I bite the inside of my cheek, scooping up my bag. I head towards the way we entered earlier, Patrick just ahead of me.

"You know, for the record," Nathan sings out, and we turn to face him. He's remarkably calm now that he's been relieved of his binds. "I only gave Kali a little bit, but she didn't need it. That slut would've opened her legs for me if you hadn't come along."

I hear Patrick sigh, "Fuck" as I swiftly cross the room and lunge at Nathan, reaching out my knife and slicing straight across the top of his left hand. A roar starts from his throat, but I slap my hand across his mouth, stifling it.

"Say that again and see what I slice through next," I seethe.

Nathan's eyes water, the vein in his forehead pulsating. A part of me wants to take little slices of him until he's begging for mercy, make him experience fear and panic like he inflicted on those women.

"Anthony." Patrick's voice is a calm and steady reminder that we're not here to go too far. That we have lives and people we care about. That was the main reason I asked him to come along. To make sure I didn't lose control.

"Don't make a fucking sound you piece of shit," I spit, removing my hand.

Nathan gasps as I release him, clutching his hand to his chest. As much as I want to beat him to a pulp, I refrain. I march across the room to scoop up my bag, passing my brother and stepping out into the frigid night once again. Patrick follows me back to the car and it's not until we've pulled out of the street that we both take several deep exhales.

"You need to get rid of that knife," Patrick remarks quietly.

The remainder of the drive is in silence, our breaths gradually slowing to a point of normality by the time we arrive back home. Patrick kills the engine as we pull into the safety of the garage.

"You okay?" Patrick asks, staring straight ahead.

I nod. "Yeah."

Surprisingly, I am. It's not the first time I've lashed out violently at someone, but it's the first time I don't feel any sort of remorse about it. That piece of shit deserves so much worse than a punch to the face and a cut on the hand.

"Thank you," I add. "For doing that with me. It won't become a habit."

Patrick gives me a small smile, unbuckling his seatbelt. "I know it won't. You don't need to explain, Anthony. Kali is important to me too."

I smile back and we both climb out of the car and head inside.

We'll never talk about this again, just like the other times. I'll get rid of the evidence and clean the car, and Patrick will keep an eye on Nathan's movements, but it'll never come up again unless it has to, which it shouldn't. We were careful, methodical and Patrick kept a clear head, saving us from any real problems. Nathan's not going to blab about it either. He's too much of a coward and we've got too much on him for him to risk it.

I grab an ice pack from the freezer and hold it against my raw knuckles, pulsating from the punch from earlier. Even if it turned out my hand was broken, it was worth it. Worth it to see the fear and to shake him up a bit. Worth it to know that he's not going to be around to bother Kali anymore and will hopefully be smart enough to change his behaviour wherever he goes to next.

Tonight, was worth every ounce of risk and if I'm honest with myself, it was a wake-up call.

I would burn the world to protect Kali.

30

KALI

I'VE WATCHED the footage from the studio camera four times now. It's dangerous having instant access to this sort of stuff on my phone. It's addictive.

The audio isn't working, but I can tell from the repeated plays that Anthony accosted the three teenage boys and ultimately convinced them to clean off their graffiti. The boys seemed resigned to something Anthony said to them as they left. Whatever he did, it has me bouncing around the studio the next day. It's a weight lifted off my shoulders.

When Hazel comes by to measure the space for the signage towards the end of the day, I show her the footage.

Hazel nods her approval once I stop the tape, opening her laptop to jot something down. "One hundred percent illegal, but impressive. Definitely a Bonetti."

"And *look* at this new entryway." I smile at the work of art that is my studio entrance.

Instead of walking straight into the studio once the roller door is lifted, visitors are greeted with a cute shopfront, complete with windows and a stained-glass door. I wanted clients to feel like they were walking into an oasis of the mind, and to be able to shut off from the noise outside without having to cage us in with the heavy roller door.

"Anthony *made* this," I gush. "With his bare hands."

Hazel smiles up at the frame. "He really is talented—"

"The amount of work he put into it is crazy. It's so beautiful."

Hazel looks at me incredulously, snapping her laptop shut with a resounding *click*. "You *like* him."

A laugh mixed with a scoff escapes my lips. "No, I don't."

"Oh my god, you *do*. Kalina Cooper!" Hazel cries.

Heat races to my cheeks. "Shut up."

"You don't catch feelings."

"I *haven't*."

Hazel taps her chin. "I mean, I guess you were a bit school-girl-ish with Alex, but that was short-lived—"

"He doesn't feel that way about me!"

It's Hazel's turn to scoff. "Did he say that?"

"Yes."

"What were his words, exactly?"

I think back to the past few weeks, focusing in on the day we decided to keep things low key between us. "We established rules about keeping things uncomplicated and unofficial. He was down with that."

She shakes her head. "You mean, *you* established rules and he agreed."

I blink at her. Did he ever say he wasn't interested in more than sex? I replay that first conversation in my head. I remember all the moments we've spent in the studio together. Our first date on the mountain and the time we spent running around the arcade. The way he looked at me in the photo booth.

The way I *felt* when he looked at me.

"Oh no." My hands cover my mouth with the realisation.

Hazel's eyes are wide with knowing. *I told you so* is written all over her stupid face.

My stomach tightens.

I've been so sure of the type of person I am for so many years, the thought of going against what I thought I knew is jarring. At this stage of the dating game, I'm bored, or at least, looking elsewhere, but thinking about it, I haven't been interested in another person since I met Anthony. The thought of bringing another person into the mix spikes jealousy. The image of another woman touching Anthony makes my blood boil.

I back away from the entryway, as if being near Anthony's latest handiwork will somehow make it more real. "No, no, no. This is wrong. I can't like him."

Hazel laughs kindly. "Why not?"

"He's like *me*. He's not into monogamy."

"Except he hasn't seen anyone since he started seeing you."

"We don't know that," I argue.

"Are you blind?" Hazel cries. "Any time he's not working he's spending it with you; helping you get the studio up and running, building you an entry way, taking you out. You are delusional if you can't see what the rest of us can."

My feet take on a life of their own, pacing up and down the room as a rush of unfamiliarity sweeps over me.

I *like* him.

I like Anthony.

Hazel notices my spiral, because her smile fades. "Don't panic."

"Too late."

"Kali, focus. This isn't a bad thing."

Heat prickles at my chest, spreading across my skin to my neck. "It doesn't feel like a *good* thing—"

"Hey Jonesy! I didn't know you'd be here."

We turn to see the man of my dreams and nightmares walking through the new front door. The soundproofing on the new frame blocked out the sound of his truck, giving me zero warning. Zero chance to prepare for my visceral reaction to seeing his painted arms contorting in the setting sunlight as he walks in. No way to ready myself for the dimple in his chin or his high cheekbones or his cheeky grin.

I have no chance to steady myself.

My newfound discovery about my goddamned feelings made me forget Anthony was coming by tonight.

But why wouldn't he be here? He's here every night, because you spend all your time together.

I'm having a breakdown.

Anthony smiles brightly at Hazel, before his gaze lands on me. He gives me a small wink and I want to melt into a puddle.

"Great timing, Anthony," Hazel says, breaking through my stupor. "I was here to finish up measurements for the signage. I'm just leaving."

My mouth drops open to stop her, but she shoots me a glare so fierce I stop myself.

"Good seeing you, Jonesy," he says with a lazy smile.

Hazel departs quickly and we're alone. Which isn't unusual, but suddenly it's all I can focus on. Anthony doesn't seem to notice my internal combustion.

"I'm secretly glad she's gone. I've got something for you," he says, backing towards the door again. "Wait here."

I barely nod, frozen to the spot as I wait for him.

He returns moments later, heaving a massive piece of timber through the door. He leans it up against the wall and stands back.

"What do you think?" Anthony beams at me, his arms outstretched towards the wooden carving.

"It's beautiful," I whisper.

It's bigger than Patrick's enormous plasma television, a thick base of timber layered with intricate designs and carvings. The patterns twirl and lace together to create the most perfectly balanced and symmetrical mandala design I have ever seen.

"I thought maybe you could hang it above the couch," he

suggests, waving to the blank space on the wall of the waiting area.

I can barely process the wonder of the art or the excitement on Anthony's face, because the noise in my ears is deafening. The constriction in my throat is unbearable. I reach my hand around my neck, battling an inexplicable panic creeping up my spine.

"The look on your face says you're not as stoked about this as I thought you'd be." Anthony is watching me, his brows furrowed with concern.

"I'm never going to be Chloe."

Anthony visibly recoils. "What?"

Ash fills my mouth. "Stop trying to repent or fix whatever issues you have with me. I'm not Chloe."

Anthony scoffs with disbelief. "I *know* you're not."

"Are you sure about that?" Blood rushes to my ears, rage surges through my veins. "Because ever since I met you, it's like you're trying to project your past onto me."

Anthony's surprise is evident by his raised eyebrows. "Wow."

A heavy silence falls between us and the need to claw out of my skin suffocates me. I have to get out of here.

I begin my march across the room towards the only available exit, but Anthony's too quick. As I open the door, he reaches his hand above my head and slams it shut. "Don't you dare run away."

His body crowds the right side of mine, but I can't look at him. I stare ahead, out of the glass panes towards the car park, focusing on breathing out of my nostrils.

"I made that because I wanted to do something for you," Anthony says, his voice steady. "You need something for the waiting area and I'm good with my hands. It's not a big deal."

I turn to face him, my chin tilted up. "How many people have you made pieces for?"

Anthony's jaw tics. "You're the test run. I haven't been crafting for that long and needed the practice."

I fold my arms and they brush against his torso. "Really? So, this has nothing to do with your feelings towards me? Nothing to do with you breaking the rules?"

Anthony's mouth curls into a lazy smile, a sneer even, as he towers above me. "Get over yourself and your stupid fucking rules."

I narrow my eyes at him. "Get out of my studio."

He leans down, so our mouths are inches apart. "What are you so afraid of?"

My breath catches at his words. I try to tear my eyes away from his, the way his search mine for answers. But I'm glued to the spot.

Hazel's words about me liking Anthony force their way into my mind. Mocking me. Shouting at me. Doing their best to take over all sense of logic and force me to succumb to them. To succumb to the idea that I do in fact have feelings for this man. So much so it terrifies me.

I see the moment Anthony recognises something in my panicked expression. He reaches back and curls his hand into the hair at the nape of my neck, tugging downwards so my chin tilts up. The sensation borders on the edge of pleasure and pain and a gasp escapes my lips.

"I hate you," I insist.

"Liar." His hand closes around my throat in a vice-like grip as his mouth devours me, his tongue plunging into my soul as if to claim it. To claim *me*.

There's nothing gentle about the way we attack each other. Teeth and nails and shoves and pulls while we try to close the distance between us. His taste is intoxicating, as if every kiss is breathing new life into me.

Anthony lifts me, his hands curving underneath me and my legs lock around his waist. With purpose, he strides out of the studio and into the frigid night air. We reach his truck and I hear the groan of the tray-door as he lowers it, our kiss never breaking. It's thrilling how Anthony moves my body with such ease, how he could throw me around if he wanted to.

He lowers me onto something comfortable.

"You put a mattress in your truck," I murmur against his lips. "Like a serial killer."

"I planned on taking you stargazing tonight, but you had to ruin everything, as usual." Anthony manoeuvres me so I'm lying on the makeshift bed, complete with comfortable bedding and pillows. "I wanted to fuck you in a field under the stars so nobody would hear you scream, but this'll have to do."

A thrill runs through my veins as he lowers his body on top of mine, his breathing ragged as he encases my head with his forearms. The idea that I drive him as crazy as he drives me turns me on even more.

He kisses me again, his mouth prying mine open hungrily. His hardness presses against me and I grind up against him, desperate for friction to ease some of my frustration. We tear each other's clothes off with ease and my skin breaks out in goosebumps at the exposure to the winter air.

The burn of the cold is momentary. Every touch from Anthony sends heat racing through me like wildfire. He pauses only for a beat to put on a condom, and then slides into me, the two of us groaning into the night air.

Who knows how many people in the vicinity hear my screams.

I don't care.

31

KALI

"You were going to take me stargazing?"

"Yep." Anthony grazes my arm under the warmth of the thick blanket, the stars doing their best to twinkle against the haze of the city lights. "This isn't a bad back-up plan though. Think your neighbours minded?"

He chuckles to himself and plants a kiss on my forehead, staring up at the sky as my gaze bores into the side of his face. I relish the banter between us. The sex is incredible. But lying up against his warm, naked flesh, *snuggling*, not having anywhere to be ... this is what fills me the most.

A wave of unfamiliar emotion washes over me, and I take in an audible breath, loud enough for Anthony to turn his attention towards me. "Cold?"

"I'm good," I croak. I make to roll away, but he stops me with his arms.

"Don't," he whispers.

I look past the blue whirlpools of magic, willing me to meet his gaze. "I can't do this."

"Why not?"

Because I can't.

Because I'm too fucked up to have a deep connection with someone.

I lift a shoulder in a shrug, biting my bottom lip to stop the tremble.

Because I'm terrified.

"Kali," he whispers, stroking the side of my face. "Look at me."

The sound of my name, not a nickname or a frustrated groan, melts my insides. I let out a shaky breath and force my gaze to meet his, my stomach flipping the minute I see his eyes.

"Whatever you're feeling right now, it's okay." Anthony's tone is a low hum of reassurance. "I'm sorry if I broke your rules. This doesn't have to be anything other than what you want it to be."

"Where did you come from?"

"From your wildest dreams."

"Oh, shut up."

Anthony grabs my wrist to stop me from playfully hitting him and rolls his naked body over mine. His hand drifts up near my cheek and a flash of red jumps out at me. "What happened to your hand?"

He grins. "You should see the other guy."

"Bonetti—"

"Stop deflecting," he orders, brushing a strand of hair out of my eyes. "You're the most beautiful woman I've ever met. Inside and out."

"Anthony, don't—"

"Take the compliments. Believe what I am saying. I know you're not into relationships and I'm telling you I don't care. I'm not a sappy guy and I'm not always great with my words, but you are a wonder, Kali."

Something boils from the depths of my belly, reaching my eyes and mouth, and an unexpected sob escapes my lips. Anthony leans down and presses his lips to my forehead while tears stream down my face. He strokes the side of my face. He runs his hands through my hair. He lets my emotions pour out until I don't have any tears left to give.

"Why aren't you scared?" I whisper, hating the sound of vulnerability in my voice.

"Who said I'm not scared?" He gives me a small smile. "I'm shitting myself. But you're worth it. I'd rather give it a go and have you break my heart than not try at all."

"It's not your heart I'm worried about."

Anthony's eyes flare with heat and something else I can't recognise. Before he can say anything, I reach up and pull his lips to mine.

It feels different this time. The moving of our lips is gentle and slow. The moving of our bodies together is careful and drawn-out, the roughness from earlier nowhere to be found. Anthony's hands roam my body, as if he's memorising the shape of it. It's only a matter of minutes before I'm desperate for him again.

He shifts on top of me, murmuring into my mouth, "Let me get a condom."

"I don't want one."

Anthony stills, blinking down at me.

"I don't want one if you don't," I clarify, nerves swirling in my gut. "I'm on birth control."

Unspoken words of trust and understanding pass between us. I note the roll of Anthony's throat as he nods. "Are you sure?"

"Yes."

Anthony exhales a shaky breath before taking my mouth again, exploring every inch. My hands curl around the back of his head and as he lines up at my entrance, I take a deep breath. He holds my gaze as he pushes himself in, watching me as I adjust to him.

"Jesus," he grunts, his head falling onto my shoulder.

Anthony's voice is hoarse as he whispers my name repeatedly, slowly sliding in and out of me. "This feels amazing. *You feel amazing.*"

It's as if he reached into my chest and squeezed my heart with his fist. It's a mixture of warmth and fear and anxiety that swirls in my gut and to every limb as he makes love to me under the stars. Again, silent tears roll down my cheeks as he fills me to the hilt repeatedly.

I'm falling for the way he speaks and moves. The way he drinks me in and looks me up and down.

I'm falling for the way he puts up with my mood swings and makes me laugh.

I'm falling for the way he's helped me day and night, to make my studio come to life.

I'm falling ...

Falling ...

My vision goes white with starlight as Anthony collapses in a heap on top of me, our sweaty bodies entangled. My heart thunders in my chest.

I'm falling for Anthony Bonetti.

32

ANTHONY

I'M A MAN RE-BORN.

Well, I don't believe in that hippy shit, but Kali does, and she could tell me mermaids exist and I'd believe her.

Last night was amazing. Better than amazing. Something shifted between the two of us. It started out with heat and anger and ended with the two of us vulnerable and exposed. I cuddled her in my truck for hours and drove her home before the sun came up. She let me walk her to the door and kiss her goodbye. She *moaned* into my mouth before I left and looked at me like she was happy.

That's how I feel. *Happy.*

Elated.

Fucking flying.

Sonny and Jared have given me shit all day. Even Bill surprised me when he grunted, "You look like an idiot in love."

I've been so nauseatingly chipper I decide to show them photos of the studio, a sense of pride for Kali and myself trumping any sort of reservations I had about sharing the hard work we've put in.

"Jesus, Peaches. When do you sleep?" Jared asks, looking over Sonny's shoulder at my phone.

I laugh. "The studios pretty much done. I can go back to early nights again."

Sonny frowns at the phone. "What the hell are these?"

For a split second I panic, wondering if I'd inadvertently left an embarrassing selfie or any evidence of my late-night attack on the graffiti boys on my camera roll. I relax when I realise Sonny's looking at the photos I took of Kali's mandala piece, and some others I'm working on in my workshop.

"Mate." Sonny takes a long pause, squinting as he scrolls through the photos. "These are bloody beautiful."

He's got the same look on his face that Patrick gets when he looks at my artwork. It's wonder mixed with respect. That's not an ego thing—I can see it in the way they go quiet, how their eyes narrow to focus on the detail.

"You made these?" Jared asks, peering over Sonny's shoulder.

"Yep."

"Jesus," Jared mutters. "You're wasting your talent here."

Bill grunts from the corner.

"They're mostly from templates I bought," I say dismissively. "I've only designed a couple of them myself."

"How much are you charging for these?" Sonny asks, zooming in on one of the photos.

I frown. "I'm not. I'm just playing around."

"Mate, you should be making these and charging good coin," he insists. "You could commission pieces for people. I want to buy one."

"Shut up."

"I'm serious." He hands me my phone back. "Can you make one for my mum? She would love something like this."

I wait to see if he's going to make a joke, but he waits for my response expectantly.

"Have a think about how much you want to charge," he adds. "I'll get you the cash later today to show you I'm serious."

Jared lets out a whistle and holds out his phone to me. He's jumped online and an image of another artist's work pops up. "This one is nearly six hundred bucks and it's nowhere near as good as yours."

"I was thinking at least a grand," Sonny says with a shrug.

"A grand?" I sputter.

"Think about how many hours it'd take you. The materials. The design. Artist's charge whatever their time's worth. Plus, you're an apprentice. You make a pittance."

"True enough," I grunt.

"I want one similar to this." He holds my phone out to me, showing me Kali's mandala.

"It's taken me a couple of months," I warn him.

He nods. "All good. I can give it to my mum for Christmas. That should be enough time, yeah?"

"Wait a minute—"

"Don't start on me, Peaches," Sonny cuts in. "Will you do it, or not?"

I nod in earnest. "I'll do it."

"Great. I'll get you some cash today."

"How about you pay me a deposit and the rest when I deliver it to you?" I suggest.

Sonny nods and reaches out, grabbing my hand to shake it. "Done."

We get back to work and the realisation that someone saw my art and wanted to put money down with barely any questions feels weird. But exciting-weird, like what I'm doing might be good. That maybe I could make a living off a hobby that's been such a constant for me in sobriety.

I don't know if this week could get any better.

33

KALI

"Do you want to bang on a reformer?"

I giggle. "I don't know how comfortable that'll be, but we can give it a try."

Anthony groans at my response, kissing me gently on the lips.

I want to kiss him all the time. He's become addictive and I wonder if I'm a little bit addictive to him. We spent all night having sex in his truck and parted ways early this morning. He went to work on minimal sleep and came here straight after, insisting on helping me put the Pilates equipment together.

We've barely touched the reformers, but we've touched each other a lot.

"You're making it impossible to concentrate," I groan, looping my arms around his neck.

He buries his face into my neck and inhales, squeezing me to him. "You're one to talk."

"We can bang on the next reformer we set up," I promise, leaning back to look at him.

His wicked grin sends heat to the space between my thighs.

"Deal. Can you grab my toolbox out of the tray? Your tools are shit."

"How dare you." I smirk at him and plant a chaste kiss on his lips.

I head out to Anthony's truck and pop the tray, sliding his toolbox to me. The lid isn't locked, and I thank my lucky stars I noticed before grabbing it by the handle. There would've been shit everywhere.

I open it to readjust the tools and notice the reason for it not closing is an envelope. The envelopes not sealed, and I see straight away there's a wad of cash inside. Easily several hundred dollars in fifty-dollar bills.

My stomach revolts, something crashing like a tidal wave in the depths of my soul. It can't be what I think it is. Anthony's been straight for years. He's got a great apprenticeship and has established a new life here. He wouldn't be doing shady shit. Would he?

I've never feared confrontation. If anything, I thrive on it, especially when I know I'm in the right. I call people out on their bullshit, and I expect the same in return. Right now, is no different, except my entire body is on fire.

Don't be reactive. Be sensible. Stay calm.

I remind myself of that as I march back inside, holding the envelope between my fingers. "Why do you have an envelope of cash in your toolbox?"

Anthony's gaze dips to the money in my hand. "Was my toolbox open?"

The fact that he doesn't answer me straight away sets alarm bells ringing in my brain. "Yes, it was."

Anthony straightens up and heads towards me, his hand outstretched with a smile. "I'm lucky shit didn't go flying when I drove here."

"What's the money for?" I ask again, my chest heaving with anticipation.

Anthony's smile fades, lowering his hand. "A friend paid me for some work."

"What sort of work?"

Anthony stares at me, unblinking for several beats. "What sort of work do you *think*?"

I sigh, frustrated. "Forget it."

Anthony sidesteps quickly and stops me pushing past him. "No, go ahead. Say whatever it is you're thinking."

The fury in his eyes is evident, but it doesn't deter me. It spurs me on. It makes me want to shout and scream and have it out with him. "Are you dealing again?"

Anthony's face breaks into a wicked smile and a chill runs through me. "Wow. You seriously went there."

"A simple yes or no would suffice."

Anthony scoffs. "Jesus, Kali."

"Why can't you answer the question?"

"Because I'm having trouble believing you're asking me that." Anthony's face looks like it could explode. "I am *not* dealing."

"Then why does it feel like you're hiding something from me? You never told me how you hurt your hand."

"Are you seriously the type of woman who needs to know my every move? Who needs to know everything that's going on in my life?" Anthony backs away from me, hooking his hands up behind his head. "If I'd known you were going to be a *possessive* girlfriend, I might've thought twice about this arrangement."

He said it to be mean, to deliberately slice into my heart.

It works.

"I'm not your girlfriend." The words feel dirty coming out of my mouth. "We've fucked a couple of times. Don't get ahead of yourself."

Anthony shakes his head in disbelief, his hands now planted on his hips. His heaving chest and pulsating jaw are his tells.

He's angry, he's *furious* and as a smile devoid of humour creeps across his face, my stomach sinks. It's one of those smiles someone gives you because they know they're in on a dirty secret or are about to deliver a punchline that'll make your soul leave your body.

"Of course." His voice drips with sarcasm. "You're not my girlfriend and never will be, right? Because you don't do feelings or relationships. Even if I'm dating or *fucking* someone else," he snarls, the emphasis on that word sending an involuntary jolt through me, "that'd be okay. Because this thing between you and me was only a bet. A bit of fun."

I clench my teeth. "Right."

"You're so full of shit."

Inexplicable rage courses through my body, the words spilling from my mouth without thought behind them. "I *told* you I didn't want anything more than that. I'm sorry you got the wrong idea."

"Are you trying to convince me or you?" Anthony tilts his head. "You're going to stand there and tell me you don't have feelings for me?"

"That's what I'm telling you," I snap.

Anthony steps forward, his eyes narrowed into slits. "*Liar.*"

"*I'm* the liar?"

"You want me to be honest?" Anthony's rage roars behind his eyes. "Here are some truths for you." He holds up his right hand, which is red and cut up. "I got this from punching Nathan in the face, moments before he admitted he drugged you and several other women with GHB, and moments after I cut his hand open with a knife."

A gasp catches in my throat, trying to process the revelations quickly, but Anthony doesn't give me time for that. His eyes gleam with rage as he keeps talking. "Want me to continue this honesty train, Kali? Let's talk about Chloe, shall we?"

The shift in his tone heightens every nerve ending in my

body. My skin prickles with warning. My throat dries. The look on Anthony's face is almost violent. Not at me, but at himself, like he wishes he didn't have to say the next words. And for a second, I want to stop him.

"Chloe didn't die because we were sitting on the couch hanging out," he says. "Chloe died because we were sitting on the couch getting *high*. With *my* stash after I suggested we do it. Me and my stupid god damned decisions are the reasons she's dead. That's why I go to therapy. That's why I don't drink, or smoke weed, or fall back onto any of the vices that got me into this fucking mess in the first place. Being an addict is bad enough, but when someone *dies* because of you, there isn't anywhere lower you can go." Anthony throws his arms in the air. "How's that for honesty? Are you happy? Now you know the whole, dirty truth."

A deafening silence settles between us as Anthony's eyes rage with fury, the sparkling in them vanishing as he stares at me. "What? Suddenly you have nothing to say?"

I struggle to form a sentence before whispering, "Why didn't you tell me?"

"Why do you think?" Anthony spits. "Because it's the biggest regret of my life."

I shake my head. "But the money—"

Anthony lets out a howl of frustration. "You're still on that? After everything I just said, you're on *that?* You know, I'm used to other people assuming the worst of me, but I never thought you'd be one of them."

Nausea comes in a giant wave that threatens to knock me to the ground; the hurt on Anthony's face almost splitting me open from the inside.

"I'm not even that upset," he continues. "Because I pity you. You need any excuse to push me away because you're a coward."

I bite the inside of my cheek. "I'm not a coward."

Anthony grits his jaw. "Yes, you are. You've made something out of nothing so you can blame our relationship failure on me and it's easier to walk away."

A scoff escapes my throat. The audacity of this man is baffling. "You really are a gifted gas lighter."

"I may have not told you the whole truth about my past, but that's because I didn't want to scare you away. But I've been nothing but honest with how I feel."

I throw my hands in the air. "That is such a load of shit! You can't pick and choose what to lie about and then claim you're doing the right thing. I might not be your version of perfect, or know what I want, but at least I'm honest about that."

"Bullshit," Anthony growls, closing the distance between us. "You've lied to me, and to yourself, since the moment I met you. I might be fucked up, but at least I'm dealing with my demons."

"Fuck you." A solitary tear slides down my cheek and I see Anthony's resolve falter.

"Kali …" He lifts a hand as if to comfort me, but I slap it away.

"I mean it. Go fuck yourself. I'm done." I snatch up my bag from the ground and march across the floor, smacking the front door open so hard it bounces off the outside wall.

34

KALI

I BARGE through the front door of my home with the force of a bison protecting its young from a pride of lions.

Hazel jumps up from the living room couch, alarmed. "What's wrong? Is everything okay?"

"No, everything is *not* okay." I hurl my bag across the room and watch it collide with a vase, smashing it to pieces.

Hazel goes rigid. "Kali, what happened?"

"Anthony fucking Bonetti!" I shout. "I am *never* speaking to that man again. My radar for fuckboys is usually at platinum level. How did I not see it with him?"

Hazel's hands remain faced out in the defensive position, like she's about to jump onto a giant crocodile and wrestle it Steve Irwin style. "What did he do?"

"He's sneaking around, being violent and *dealing* again."

Hazel's mouth drops open. "What? No. No, that can't be true."

"It's true! He told me he punched Nathan in the face and used a knife on him and I found an envelope of cash."

She furrows her brow. "A *knife?* Wait, you think the cash was from a drug deal?"

"He denied it, obviously."

"And you don't believe him?"

"No." I throw my hands in the air. "I don't know! He called me possessive and a coward. I told him to go fuck himself. I can't even remember how it all happened."

The last half hour morphs into a nightmare as I bury my face in my hands. The array of emotions I saw on Anthony's face in the time we fought play on repeat, antagonising my anxiety.

"Do you really think Anthony's dealing again?" Hazel asks. I lift my head to see concern etched into her face, but I'm too wound up to feel anything but anger towards him.

"I don't know," I snap. "But we need to ask ourselves how well we even know him. He admitted to using violence towards Nathan only after I caught him out. How do we know he hasn't been pretending to be this reformed, nice guy this whole time?"

Hazel's eyes narrow. "I know you don't think that's true."

I hear the blood rushing in my ears again, my throat constricting as I gasp for breath. All I want to do is scream again, but I can't think straight.

"Kali, breathe," Hazel orders. "I'm sure it's not as bad as you think. Anthony adores you. He's been your person for the past few months. Even *you* can admit that."

"He's not my person," I argue. "I don't want a person! I don't *need* another person to be happy."

"That's not—"

"I don't *want* another person! I'm fine not being some pathetic, heart-eyed woman obsessed with her partner and who can't function without a man in her life."

Hazel's expression glimmers from sad to annoyed. "Kali, no one is saying that."

"We slept together a couple of times, and he made me a piece of art. Big deal."

Hazel raises her eyebrows. "He made you a piece of art?"

"You're missing the point."

"And what exactly is the point?" Hazel asks, genuine bewilderment on her face.

"He shouldn't have made me the art piece!"

Hazel looks alarmed. "Why not?"

"Because it's a sign he caught feelings, and I told him I don't do those."

"Riiiiight," she draws out. "He caught feelings, and you had your first proper fight and you're upset. And maybe, you also caught feelings?"

"Oh my God, you sound just like him! I don't want to be one of those women."

"*I'm* one of those women!" Hazel cries, throwing her hands in the air. "What is so wrong with that? There's nothing wrong with allowing yourself to love someone, Kali!"

"And end up like my mother? A shell of a woman who could barely function after her soulmate died? So much so, that she checked out of reality and ultimately died from the pain?"

That look I *hated* as a child crosses Hazel's face. Pity. "Kali, you are not your mother."

Tears blur my eyes as I stare Hazel down. "And I *never* will be."

I storm out of the house before Hazel can say another word. It's not until I round the corner that sobs rip from my throat.

35

ANTHONY

I ROLL the unlit cigarette between my fingers before lifting it to my nostrils and inhaling. The smell and the way it flares up my brain before it's even lit should concern me, but I welcome it.

"You alright?"

I'm not surprised that my brother crept inside the house with the deftness of a ninja. He's stealthy at the best of times.

"Just dandy," I grunt.

Patrick remains somewhere behind me. I imagine his eyes narrowed with concern, watching his screwup younger brother sitting on the back steps, staring at the ocean and sniffing an unlit cigarette like a weirdo. "Those things will kill you, you know. What happened?"

I sigh. "Things got screwed up with Kali."

Patrick hums under his breath but says nothing.

"She found cash in my car. It was payment for an art piece from a guy at work. She immediately thought I was dealing and ... I ... I unleashed all this pent-up rage and told her how I'm responsible for Chloe's death. Might have mentioned what I did to Nathan. Safe to say, it didn't go well."

Patrick's designer shoes come into view, and he silently joins me on the steps, his hands clasped together. He squints as he too looks out at the ocean, his perfect hair waving slightly in the breeze.

"That couldn't have been pretty," he muses.

"The dealing accusation set me off," I admit. "I can't say I blame her. I kept so much from her. Why wouldn't she jump to the worst conclusion?"

I tuck the cigarette behind my ear and rub my hands down my face, hoping it'll somehow ease some of the pressure behind my cheekbones. "Why didn't I just tell Kali about Chloe when I met her? I don't know why everything's so different with her."

Patrick tuts. "You don't?"

I glance at my brother, and one of his eyebrows is already quirked in that annoying, knowing way.

My head drops into my hands. "Fuck."

"I knew it," Patrick says, triumph lacing his words. "I *knew* you were in deep."

I love Kali.

I'm *in love* with her.

And I have been since the minute I laid eyes on her.

I run my hands over my head. "I should've told her everything right from the start."

"Maybe," Patrick agrees, and I scowl at him. "But it's not something that comes up naturally over coffee the first day you meet someone. Look how long I kept things from Hazel."

"That's different. You weren't a total fuck-up."

Patrick shakes his head. "Anthony, you're not a fuck-up."

"Maybe not so much anymore."

Patrick chuckles. "You've been through some terrible things in your life, but you've come out of it all and you're better for it. You're not responsible for Chloe's death."

"Now I *know* you're lying out of your ass."

Patrick shakes his head. "I never blamed you. I was angry about the situation. Angry I wasn't there when it happened.

Angry at the world for taking her from me. But I was also grateful you weren't taken from me as well. If we hadn't lost Chloe, who knows ... maybe you wouldn't be here now."

I fish out my elastics, the urge to break something building in my fists. "You think she was taken from us, so I'd get my shit together? That's bleak."

Patrick doesn't answer. I wrap my hands around the pink material and pull so it digs into my skin. "I suggested we get high. I knew she was battling her own addiction, and I didn't care."

I glance at Patrick who's watching me. "Remember what Chloe used to always say about addiction?"

"What?"

"We don't choose to be addicted; what we choose to do is deny our pain." Patrick's lips lift into a small smile. "She was hurting, Anthony. She was using all the time. No matter how much I tried to help her, she was on her own destructive path. If she hadn't done it with you, she would've done it soon after anyway."

"But she—"

"And if she hadn't joined you on the couch, maybe the car would've hit *you*," Patrick cuts in. "Maybe you'd be dead, and she'd be alive, battling with the guilt and shame of it all, just as you have."

"She deserves to be here more than I do," I mutter.

Patrick shifts, turning towards me. "You have to stop blaming yourself for the past, Anthony. Let it go. Let *Chloe*, go. You deserve to be here."

He squeezes my shoulder before standing and heading inside.

It's simultaneously peaceful and chaotic, listening to the waves crash on the rocks below whilst battling the thoughts in my brain. The twirling of the elastics causes friction on my knuckles, and I welcome it. Not in a morbid way, but as a reminder I'm still here. In flesh and blood and life.

Maybe my brother's right. Maybe I *do* deserve to be here. I've spent the past four years working hard to convince everyone else that I do. My family, my friends, people in NA, my therapist, my new boss.

Kali.

Somehow, amongst all the healing and hard work I forgot to check in with myself. I've been happy lately, but I've never consciously thought about how happy I am to be alive. To be where I am. I've never given myself time to stop and revel in it.

Despite the weight of the fight with Kali weighing on my chest, I smile. The fact that I can process events like this and not think about reaching for money to buy drugs, is a vast cry from where I was a few years ago.

I stand up and head back inside, grabbing my car keys with a plan of attack.

I'm going to go to an NA meeting. If I need to be around anyone right now, its fellow addicts trying to stay clean.

Then, I'm going to smoke the cigarette curled around my ear.

And once I've done those two things, I'll allow myself to think about how everything went so poorly with the woman I fell head over heels in love with.

36

KALI

MIMI DIDN'T ASK me what was wrong when I let myself into her house. She stayed seated in her favourite armchair, reached an arm out and beckoned me to her. I collapsed on the floor and put my head in her lap and haven't moved since.

My tears have stopped, and the low hum of a familiar song comes from Mimi's throat as she strokes my hair. "Do you want to talk about it?"

A thousand thoughts race through my mind, triggering a thousand emotions. I can't pinpoint what even happened. Anger, shame, fear, embarrassment, guilt scream from my brain and through my veins. I lean back to look at her, my neck aching from resting in the same position for so long.

"I know that look," she says, smiling fondly. "You're in love."

I squeeze my eyes shut, but fresh tears roll down before I can stop them. Mimi's thumb wipes them from my face. "This is a *wonderful* thing, Kiki."

I open my eyes at the mention of my childhood nickname and smile. "It doesn't feel like it."

"Did he hurt you?"

A flurry of thoughts whizz through my mind. Of how much Anthony has helped me. How he's protected me one minute and made me laugh the next. He's allowed me to be myself, made me feel alive. I might've been upset before, but the reality that I completely jumped the gun is settling in.

I shake my head. "I hurt *him*."

Mimi smiles. "Nothing that can't be fixed, Kalina."

I lower my head in shame. "I said some awful things and acted like a brat. No, I acted like an *asshole*. He'll never want to speak to me again. I don't deserve him."

"Sounds like you're letting your passion for life get in the way of experiencing joy," Mimi murmurs.

I scoff and snot runs from my nose. "You can't help yourself, can you?"

"Let me tell you something, Kalina. I would rather have an all-consuming, can't-live-without-you kind of love and live with the pain of the aftermath, than never experience it at all. When you find true love, it's worth every ounce of the pain."

"Did you have that with Baba?"

She smiles, the lines in her face wrinkling around her eyes. "Our love was magic and despite the pain of not having him all this time, I wouldn't change a single thing."

"I don't want to end up like mum," I admit.

Mimi nods, a sadness on her face. "It's normal to have that fear, Kiki. Sometimes love can be the most painful thing we ever experience. Some people can cope, and some people can't. Your mother was broken-hearted, and she pushed everyone away. She cut everyone off, even you, because she didn't feel worthy of this life without your father."

Mimi takes a quiet breath and I squeeze her hand. This is the first time we've ever talked about this openly and I realise I'm not the only one who this has haunted. She lost her son without warning; she couldn't save her daughter-in-law and her rock passed away before his time.

"We're all made differently," she says, giving me a sweet smile. "We all cope differently, and *you* will survive, no matter what happens. I can feel it here." She thumps a fist to her chest and more silent tears stream down my face.

"What if he destroys me?" I whisper.

"What if he doesn't?"

The weight of those words hangs over my head as I let the tears roll without shame. Mimi continues to run her hand through my knotted hair as we contemplate our thoughts.

"What do I do?" I finally ask, leaning back to look up at her.

Mimi smiles, wrinkles creasing her face. "You already know, Kalina."

Hazel's banging about in the kitchen when I walk back into the house that night. Spices and soy sauce waft through my nostrils and I take a deep breath, my figurative tail between my legs as I walk through the entrance.

Her heads lifts as I enter, relief flickering across her face. She walks over and pulls me in for a hug just as I start wittering away with my apologies.

"I'm sorry."

Hazel gives me a squeeze. "Me too."

"What are you apologising for?"

"I yelled at you."

I chuckle into her shoulder. "I deserved it."

"Are you alright?"

I shrug. "Who knows? I've got to go back to therapy."

Hazel barks out a laugh. "Me too." She steps back and raises an eyebrow. "You owe me a new vase."

I snort. "I'll replace it first thing tomorrow."

"You'd better." Hazel laughs. "It cost four dollars from the cheap shop. Have you spoken to Anthony?"

The mere mention of his name makes me sick. "He won't want anything to do with me. I was an absolute psycho."

"I'm sure it wasn't that bad."

"Remember when I got drunk at Blues on Broadbeach and had an argument with a table of people eating lamb?"

Hazel's eyes widen and she tilts her head. "Oh, dear."

"Yah." I close my eyes and exhale a huge sigh. "I don't have time to make a fool of myself again anyway. The studio opens in a month. I've got to finish setting up the equipment, hire staff and get the signage on the wall."

"Yes, and you can busy yourself with tasks all you like," Hazel agrees. "But eventually, you'll realise you need to fix things with Anthony. I think addressing that sooner rather than later would be best."

"There's no way he'll respond to messages or calls right now. I royally messed up."

"Then make him listen to you." Hazel's eyes blaze with determination. "Don't let months go between the two of you, wondering what you could've done to fix things earlier. Don't waste time, Kali."

I know she's referring to the months that passed between her and Patrick before they reunited earlier this year. Although the time helped Hazel focus on herself, it chewed her up every day, not knowing what happened and not fighting harder for answers.

"Tomorrow," I promise her. "First thing tomorrow I will fix this."

I just have to hope it's not too late.

37

KALI

BRIGHT AND EARLY THE next morning, I knock on the door three times before I can talk myself out of it. When the door swings open, I frown at the sight of an expensive business shirt.

"You could at least pretend you're excited to see me." Patrick smirks as he widens the door. "Come in."

I step inside and head to the open kitchen, taking a second to appreciate the breath-taking view of the ocean before turning to him. "Is Anthony here?"

"No, sorry. He left before the sun was up this morning."

Disappointment floods my veins. "Do you know where he is?"

"I'm not checking in on him as often as I used to. He deserves my trust." Patrick folds his arms as he leans against the kitchen counter, observing me. "He deserves yours too, Kali."

Tears spring to my eyes before I can stop them. I'm an idiot. A hot-headed, dramatic, ridiculously stupid, soon-to-be-crying, *idiot*.

Patrick surprises me by reaching out and swiftly pulling me

into a side hug. The act of kindness sets off the pooling tears and they cascade down my face as I stare at the floor, willing them to stop.

"I don't say that to upset you," Patrick says quietly, rubbing my back. "You've been a shining light to my brother the past few months. He's happier than I've seen him in years."

I wipe a wayward tear, biting the inside of my cheek until I taste blood. "But I ruined it."

Patrick shakes his head. "You didn't ruin anything. No one can blame you for being wary of Anthony's behaviour. Hell, it's taken me years to stop babysitting him." Patrick sighs, his frown deepening. "But he doesn't need a babysitter. He needs his brother to trust him. He needs his friends to treat him as an equal. He needs *you* to believe the good in him and not jump to conclusions because he's made some questionable decisions in his life. *Extremely* questionable."

Patrick's words sting, but I don't lash out and bite back like I normally would, because he's right. Anthony opened up to me, trusted me, put everything out on the table. And how did I repay him? By immediately getting suspicious and not listening to his side of the story. I accused him of dealing and shattered everything we'd built in a matter of seconds.

Wringing my hands together, I take some deep breaths. I concentrate on my breathing and use that as an anchor to stop myself from spiralling. I know Patrick's watching me, but I'm not bothered. I don't care how stupid I look. I need to calm down so I can think clearly and figure out what to do next.

"You know him better than you think," Patrick says. He gives me a nod of encouragement "Where would he go to help him think straight? A place which brings him comfort?"

It takes me a few seconds before I'm hugging my thanks to Patrick and flying out the door.

I reach the top of Mount Tamborine and pull into a parking space. A couple of hang gliders are out, with two more getting ready to run and jump. There's every chance Anthony came and went in the time it took me to get up here. Driving up the windy roads in my beat-up old car alone, was nowhere near as fun as when Anthony had driven us.

I search the area before my eyes land on the sinewy frame under a tree, standing with his hands tucked into his pant pockets as he watches the gliders fly over the cliff face.

I make my way to him, wringing my hands as I imagine every worst-case scenario. What if he blows up at me, or worse, he ignores me and walks away? What if I blurt out something hurtful and stupid like I did last time?

He must sense me standing nearby, because his gaze leaves the gliders to land on me. For the tiniest moment, he locks up, almost as if he can't believe I'm there, but it fades as quickly, and I wonder if I've imagined it. "Figures you'd find me."

"It didn't come to me straight away," I reply, moving to stand beside him.

The two of us look at the devastatingly beautiful view, the morning sun blaring down on the hill as several hang gliders swerve in and out of each other.

"Did you know the longest hang-gliding flight lasted eleven hours?" Anthony asks.

"No, I didn't know that. How did they pee?"

Anthony's mouth twists, but he doesn't look at me. The energy between us is tense and uncomfortable.

I hate it.

"What're you doing here, Kali?"

"I came to apologise."

He still hasn't looked back at me. "For what? You were only ever yourself and you gave me the facts upfront. You can't apologise for that."

He's matter of fact and grown-up and *cold*. I hate this side of him. What's worse is that *I'm* responsible for bringing this side out. For unfairly assuming he was up to no good and acting like an idiot.

"I'm sorry." Anthony blinks, so I take that as my cue to continue. "In case you hadn't noticed, I'm irrational and hotheaded and I tend to disregard most people in my life unless they've been in it for longer than a few months." I take a sharp inhale and breathe it out deliberately. "I'm ashamed of the things I said and thought. I should've acted like an adult and spoken to you about it calmly. I'm sorry for being crazy."

Anthony glances at me. "Possibly, but you're not a bad type of crazy, Kali. You own who you are. Don't apologise for who you are."

I reach out and rest a hand on his flexed forearm and he turns to look at me. "But that's *not* who I am. Not anymore."

Anthony's eyes flash with something, but he doesn't speak. "Since you came into my life, I've felt happier and safer than I have in years. I've been able to be completely myself. But I didn't know how to deal with that, and it wasn't until I lost it the other day, and took it out on everyone else, that I realised I've got some serious issues to deal with. One being my inability to give myself over to a good thing. Especially when it's right in front of me."

Anthony surveys me and relief floods through me when he reaches for my hand and gives it a squeeze.

"You are that good thing, Anthony." My vision blurs. "And if you'll let me, I'd like to see if it can become something great."

Anthony sighs. "Kali—"

"Oh, god." I swallow the urge to vomit and wipe my eyes.

"No, no, stop panicking," Anthony assures me. He pushes my hair behind my ear and touches my cheek. "All I ever wanted was for you to give us a chance. To admit to yourself, maybe you do like this guy. But I would never push you into something you're not ready for."

Relief floods through my veins. "I know you wouldn't. None of this had anything to do with you. Turns out I've got some serious shit I need to work on." I take a deep breath. "I'm going back to therapy."

Anthony tilts his head, a small smile peeking out at the corners of his mouth. "It was for a commissioned piece."

I blink a few times, unsure if I've heard him correctly. "I'm sorry?"

"The money. A guy from work paid me in cash to create an art piece for his mum's birthday."

Embarrassment and shame course through my veins. "Shit."

"And for the record, I knew you were crazy the moment I laid eyes on you," Anthony smirks.

"Hey, you're no saint in this you know," I argue, pointing my finger at him. "You lied to me."

Anthony's mouth twists. "I omitted some truths."

"How about you start with what happened with Nathan?"

Anthony shakes his head. "Patty and I agreed you don't need to worry about that."

"So, Patrizio is involved?"

Anthony smirks. "Whoops. Anyway, don't get all high and mighty, you're a liar too."

"No, I'm not!"

"Oh, really? So, all that shit about not caring about me and this being a fling? That was the truth?" Anthony steps closer, leaning down so we're inches apart. "Are you telling me you're not my girlfriend?"

My heart thunders in my chest. My initial instinct is to rage. To blow up. To shout expletives at him and tell him he doesn't know anything about me.

But that's not what I want to do. It's not how I want to react or feel. That's what I revert to because of past trauma, because of who I thought I wanted to be.

That's not me anymore.

"Are you saying you'll still have me as your girlfriend?" I ask quietly.

Anthony's face breaks with his cheeky smile and his arms encircle me, pulling me flush to him.

I lean into his chest and sigh, inhaling his crisp scent. "This might be insane. We argue a lot."

Anthony tips my chin back to get a better look at me. "We bicker."

"We *fight*. It's not healthy."

Anthony shrugs. "Says who?"

"Says people. Says society. Fighting all the time isn't healthy."

Anthony shakes his head. "Where are you getting these rules from?"

I step back from him. "Why do I have to love someone who makes me want to strangle him at every waking minute? *Why?*"

It's not until the silence hits me that I realise what I said.

Anthony is staring at me. "What did you say?"

"Nothing."

Anthony's blue eyes are wide with wonder as he edges closer to me again. "What did you say, Kali?"

"I didn't…I don't know, I was talking, and I said a lot of stuff."

"You said you love me."

My body locks up. "No, I didn't."

Anthony's grin widens. "You did."

"That doesn't sound like something I would say."

Anthony clucks his tongue, smugness oozing out of his face. "You said it because you love me."

I throw my hands in the air in annoyance. "Okay, *fine!* I love you. You happy now? For fuck's sake."

Anthony's eyes flare, his smiling fading. "Say it again."

"I love you."

"I win." He grabs the back of my head and pulls me to his mouth, sucking the oxygen out of my body as I melt into him. "And I love you too, you absolute lunatic."

38

KALI

"THE FLOWER PEOPLE broke down at the intersection in Broadbeach!" Meg screams.

The sun hints at breaking over the horizon and the studio is chaos. Meg appointed herself project leader and is barking orders to everyone, a headpiece on her head (yes, an actual headpiece connected to her phone) and a clipboard in her arms. With the studio set to open its doors for the 'soft launch' in under an hour, anxiety is at an all-time high for everybody in the vicinity.

"Anthony is racing to help them," Meg explains breathlessly, running up to me. She glances at her clipboard with pursed lips, before waving her arms around the room. "The activewear girls are setting up in this corner and we're laying the gift bags on this table. The protein guys can go *here* and Reuben's coffee van will be out the door and to the right. He'll be here in twenty."

"Thank God. I need caffeine," Hazel groans, shuffling up to us with a box of candles. Patrick follows closely behind, holding another box. "Where are these going?"

"I want two near the sink in the bathroom," Meg replies. "And two of the same scent, not a mixture. Patrick, your box needs to go to that corner. I've got a cute pattern I want to set up."

Hazel heads off to the small bathroom at the side of the room and Patrick winks at me before turning away. Meg stands in front of me, her eyebrows pulled together in a serious frown. "Is there anything else you need? I'm going to start filming stories to post on the Gram."

"You're the best, you know that?" I pull Meg in for a hug and squeeze her.

My friends are supercharged this morning, running around and ensuring everything is perfect. I've gone over it a million times and finally feel like it's fallen into place. If people are late or don't show up, I'll know it wasn't for lack of trying by me or my amazing friends.

I release Meg and she looks at me with her most serious expression. "It's going to be great. Bookings for this morning's classes are *sold out*. Emma Parker will be here to share it with her fifty thousand followers. Your staff look amazing. There's great coffee. It will be incredible."

"Thank you. You're a bossy pain in the ass, but I've never been more grateful."

Meg gives me another squeeze before heading across the room to round up my newly hired instructors for photos.

I spin and take in the space, my heart singing with joy. It looks better than I ever imagined. Pot plants and white walls and the hanging lights set the mood. The mandala art piece Anthony created for me hangs above the sofa by the entrance, right where he suggested it should go.

I take a few seconds to plant myself firmly in the moment, to take a mental picture of what this space looks like and how it feels to have gotten here. To practice a bit of gratitude (my therapist says I need to get better at that). Naturally, as I sit in the sensations of contentment, pride and anticipation, my thoughts drift to my parents. I wonder what my dad would say. I wonder if my mum would be proud.

I think she would be.

I glance at myself in one of the ten full-length mirrors lining the northern wall. I've worn brand new activewear for the occasion. A bright pink crop and shorts with gleaming white shoes. I look every part the unbearable Gold Coast influencer and I'm so into it.

"I didn't think you could get any hotter." Anthony walks in through the door, holding two heavy-looking vases filled with lilies in his arms. The muscles in his forearms pop against the strain, but he's too busy smiling at me to seem bothered.

I turn to face him. "You've seen me in activewear. This is most of my wardrobe."

Anthony swaggers towards me and leans his face through the flowers to kiss my lips. My eyes flutter close, and a contented sigh escapes my lips.

Nope. That still hasn't gotten old.

"Yeah, but I've never seen you in activewear about to be a boss bitch and put people through workouts in your own business." Anthony kisses me again before heading to the front counter to lower the flowers.

"I'd check with Meg before you leave those there," I warn him.

"I don't answer to Meg." He places the vases down and turns back to me, curling his arms around my back, burying his face into my neck. "I answer to you. And Emma, of course."

I laugh.

Emma Parker, the Gold Coast's current 'it' influencer, purchased one of Anthony's pieces a few weeks ago after coming to check out the studio for a private "behind-the-scenes" sneak peek (again, thanks to Meg who arranged it all). Emma posted it on her social media and was flooded with questions about where she got it. As a result, Anthony has a full calendar of commissioned, one-off pieces scheduled for the next six months.

"You're going to kill it," Anthony assures me, his lips grazing underneath my ear. "I can already see how this is going to go. You'll end up taking over this entire block of warehouses because demand will be so high. There's already one available to get you started."

I lean back and frown at the mention of Nathan's now empty shop. Anthony told me everything that happened with the teenagers (who've left me alone) and Nathan, who up and vanished a matter of days after Anthony and I made up. He also told me that Patrick handed over all the information he had on Nathan to some of his former colleagues, who have since opened a police investigation into him. I'm not exactly happy with how he and Patrick handled it, but I can't deny I was turned on with how brazen he was. How he was willing to tear the world apart to protect me. He may or may not have got a thank you blowjob that day.

Patrick ended up telling Hazel (because if he didn't, I would've). She was furious with the two of them for being so reckless and told Patrick she wouldn't move in with him if he ever pulled a stunt like that again. Living by myself in our town-house for the past week has been better than I thought it'd be. I miss having Hazel there all the time, but it means Anthony and I can have sex whenever and wherever we want without consequences. I'm secretly glad he's already started leaving personal items at my place.

"I just want it to start already," I sigh. "This build-up is killing me."

"We've got some time. Want me to settle some of those nerves for you?" Anthony leans in and bites my earlobe, and I can't help the dreamy sigh that escapes my lips.

"I can't. Mimi's going to be here any minute."

"Not a problem. I can work quickly."

"Your cockiness is out of control," I murmur.

Anthony leans back to catch my gaze. "It's warranted. Didn't I tell you? I've very good with my hands. And my mouth."

I squeal with delight as he pulls me towards the storage cupboard, my heart roaring with love.

Crazy love, but that suits us perfectly.

EPILOGUE

Want more of Kali and Anthony?
Get access to the *Crazy Love* epilogue at
www.hannahsmithauthor.com

———

Did you enjoy *Crazy Love*? I hope so!

If you liked this book, please leave a review on Amazon or
Goodreads. Reviews are pure gold to indie authors and help our
books get noticed. Even a few words make all the difference.

Thank you.

ACKNOWLEDGEMENTS

Writing *Crazy Love* was a turbulent experience.

Don't get me wrong, some of it was magical. But a lot of it was tough. I struggled to get into my characters heads and suffered with severe burnout, big life changes and the death of a loved one. I did a lot of things to help with the creative process, the most effective being taking time away to reset. To anyone clawing their way through something—take a break. It'll be there when you get back.

I don't think there are enough words right now to thank the reading and writing communities properly. Writing can be a lonely job, but it's the people in these spaces that make you feel connected. These are the people who push you to keep going, who encourage you when you're down, who offer sound advice when you're awake at 2am pulling your hair out. From the bottom of my heart, thank you all for everything.

Thank you to my family, friends and loyal readers who've sent me words of encouragement, left reviews, and told their friends about my books. It means so much to have your support, especially on the tough days.

To my editor, Rachel Collins. I am so grateful to have you in my corner. Thank you for all your advice and most of all, your patience while I battled with this one. I'm so happy with how it turned out.

To my beta readers: Jen, Kate, Mel and Sian. I think you all understood how anxious I was about handing this one over to other people and I'm so grateful that you took time out of your busy lives to provide me with constructive feedback. Thank you.

To my amazing ARC readers. Thank you for embracing *Crazy Love* with open arms and taking the time to leave reviews. I am so grateful for each and everyone of you.

To my boys, Josh and Maxi. Thank you for everything. For supporting me, encouraging me and comforting me. I love you dearly.

Finally, I want to acknowledge my cousin, Jack Donaldson. He fought valiantly until the very end and taught me what it means to stick your middle finger up to things out of your control. Literally. Thanks, legend. We miss you.

ABOUT THE AUTHOR

Hannah Smith realised her love for writing at a young age. Her stories follow strong women on journeys of self-discovery and love, because women are bad bitches and she loves romance.

Hannah lives with her partner Josh, and their rescue dog, Maxi, on the southeast coast of Australia. When not writing, you can find Hannah watching true crime documentaries or reading a book with a cup of tea in hand.

Sign-up to Hannah's newsletter for the latest updates, sneak peeks and giveaways: www.hannahsmithauthor.com

BOOKS BY HANNAH SMITH

The Wipeout Series

The King Contract

Hazy Love Series

Hazy Love

Crazy Love

www.ingramcontent.com/pod-product-compliance
Lightning Source LLC
Chambersburg PA
CBHW032002170626
46807CB00006B/2607